I0584428

Terrorizing

Tara

'TARA' SERIES
Detective Crime Mystery

Recent Reviews

3rd book in the series
Tangle with Tara

2018 First place winner in the Texas Authors Association Contest.

A compelling third entry into a series with an irresistible appeal to fans of sleuth and crime fiction, *Tangle with Tara* by Jeri Lynn Stone follows female Detective Tara Woods on a dangerous quest to uncover and free missing teens.

Jeri Lynn Stone's literary strength lies in her ability to create characters that are real and complex and a plot that leaves readers guessing what comes next. She uses premonition to arouse the sense of fear in her readers and makes them feel as though something awful could happen any moment. The imagery in the writing is strong and it appeals to the reader's emotions in the same way it excites the imagination. The image of the young, whimpering girls with tormented eyes, six of them "bound with quarter-inch chains" that are secured to the wall is one of the powerful images that will stay with the reader and it makes for a strong opening for the story.

The dialogues reflect real human interactions and sustain the tension that moves the plot forward. I adored the skill with which this author handles character, and she does an impeccable job in letting readers see what drives her characters. The plot is tidily accomplished, and the climactic denouement leaves the readers with satisfaction. Overall, it is an emotionally charged story with great potential to entertain readers.

Divine- The Book Commentary

Amazon
https://www.amazon.com/Tangle-Tara-Mrs-Jeri-Stone/dp/1977939414
https://www.amazon.com/Tangle-Tara-Jeri-Lynn-Stone-ebook/dp/B07665ZCT7
Kobo
https://www.kobo.com/us/en/ebook/tangle-with-tara
B&N
https://www.barnesandnoble.com/w/tangle-with-tara-jeri-lynn-stone/1113573281?ean=9781977939418
Wal-mart
https://www.walmart.com/ip/Tangle-with-Tara-9780692049242/622462813

About the Author

Jeri Lynn Stone is the author of a police procedural/ detective crime mystery fiction '*Tara*', a stand-alone series. She lives in a small Arkansas town with her husband. They love to camp and fish. They live in the center of four beautiful lakes and each are within twenty-five miles from home. Both love going to antique car shows, gardening and Mother Nature. She has enjoyed writing novels, from historical to chick lit to mystery. She's currently working on the fifth novel in her Detective Crime Mystery "Tara" series, Trusting Tara.

BOOKS BY JERI LYNN STONE
<u>'TARA' DETECTIVE CRIME MYSTERY</u>
<u>SERIES</u>

TAUNTING TARA
TEACHING TARA
TANGLE WITH TARA
TERRORIZING TARA

<u>COMING NEXT</u>
TRUSTING TARA

ISBN- 9798656454179

ACKNOWLEDGEMENT

I would like to thank my wonderful husband, my family, my husband's family, friends, and the wonderful writers' communities for the loving support they've given me all of these years. I'm very grateful and honored to have everyone in my life.

I would also like to thank my terrific critique partners and editor. They keep me on the straight and narrow path in my writing career.

And, to my fans. You are the greatest. I appreciate you all.

Thank you,
Jeri Lynn Stone

CHAPTER ONE

She ran deeper into the dense woods during the darkest part of the night. Tree branches slapped her face, and vines clawed at her feet. Spooky shadows and cobwebs led her way to safety. Harsh sobs and gasping breaths racked her body and covered the sound of footsteps pounding behind her.

But, she knew they were still there.

Glancing back for an instant, she never saw the fallen log in front of her. She tripped, and landed hard on her stomach, knocking the breath out of her. Panic seized her heartbeat and slammed it hard against her chest. Her breath whooshed out between her lips in a feverish prayer. "Please, God. Please, God."

Wiping her tangled hair from the tears mingling with the fresh blood and dirt stinging her face, she rose to her torn, bare feet and stumbled forward on trembling legs, staggering and weaving her way toward freedom, away from the five days of the unbearable nightmare she'd endured, suffered and finally escaped.

She screamed out in terror as rough hands came out of the darkness and grabbed her.

* * *

At nine Monday morning, Homicide Detective Tara Woods circled a freshly dug, shallow grave. A jogger had discovered the grave earlier that morning beside a large oak tree outlying a popular park's jogging trail. He'd called it in.

Tara made precise notations in a small laptop tablet. "Victim number three. Same MO. Young woman, mid-twenties, shoulder length, black hair with a child's pink barrette pulling her bangs to the side."

Matt Dobbs, her partner of two years and the medical examiner, Ben Marks kept silent while she typed. She knew they were following along with her words while she worked the scene out in her mind.

She wanted to get a closer look. The area where the body lay had been cleared of evidence by the forensic team, so Tara knelt beside the nude body lying in the grave. Her nostrils flared. The smell of death was nauseating. She held a hand over her nose and her eyes watered.

The extreme, humid heat of the July's summer had intensified, escalating the girl's deterioration. It was already 80 degrees and the weatherman was predicting mid-nineties by evening. This part of her job never got easier. She took a shallow breath between her fingers and prayed she didn't throw up on the victim.

She'd never hear the last of it from her partner or the team. Or, forgive herself.

Noticing the forensic team methodically taking pictures, marking and bagging the evidence a few feet away, she swallowed hard and gathered her thoughts.

Removing her hand from her mouth, she continued voicing her observations to her tablet. Any and every detail could be significant to their investigation. She glanced back down at the victim. "Her hands are tied in a bow with a lacy, pink ribbon around her wrists. A bloody, thornless, pink rose was placed between her fingers. One small bullet hole right between her eyes ended her life. My guess, it was from a .22 Caliber pistol. Same as the other two victims." She turned to her partner. "What do you think, Dobbs?"

Dobbs rubbed the back of his neck. "I think it's a damn shame for a young life to end this way." He studied the naked body. "Well, we know it's not a copycat murder, since we've never let this one crucial detail made public. I believe we have us a serial killer."

Tara nodded and swallowed down the sick feeling in the pit of her stomach. This was the second serial killer case she'd worked on in the past few months. She glanced back at the dead woman and typed into her tablet before saying, "I believe so, too, and like you said, it's one hell of a way to die." She motioned with her hand to the one important detail they'd kept from the media on all three recent victims. Just like the others, this woman had been placed on her back with her legs spread wide. A long, black-haired doll, similar to the size of the Barbie doll Tara played with as a child, was pushed deep into the woman's vagina.

* * *

Around two that afternoon in front of the 13th precinct, Tara stood beside Chief Haynes and Dobbs while speaking into the microphone, giving her statement to a room full of media.

Cameras flashed as she spoke. "This is what we know so far on our latest victim. Her name is Lori Crawford. Her parents reported her missing seven days ago. She was a white female, age twenty-five, a single mother of a four-year-old son. She'd dropped him off at her parent's home around eight last Monday morning and left for work, but she never made it. Her late model Honda Civic was located two miles from the real estate agency where she worked. This morning, a jogger's dog disturbed her freshly dug, shallow grave in Oak Woods park. The medical team established she'd been deceased for less than twenty-four hours before she was found."

Looking around the room Tara took a deep breath and continued. "Based on Doctor Cindy Tablor, our profiler's initial report, we believe the murderer stalked Ms. Crawford, perhaps even knew her. He would've known her routine, what time she dropped off her son, what time she went to work. We think he's a loner who stays to himself. He's probably highly anti-social with low self-esteem. He's also extremely organized and focused. Something or someone in his life hurt him, and we believe Ms. Crawford reminded him of his pain."

Tara shrugged. "Other than the profile, we don't have much to go on. We're asking you, the public to call our hotline if you know anything or anyone who fits this description. You could help us find this guy before it happens, again. Your name will remain confidential, of course." She looked directly into the cameras with a plea. "Please, everyone, take extra precautions and always be aware of your surroundings. Now, I'll open the floor for questions."

A young, blonde, female news reporter spoke up. "Do you have any suspects? Do you think it's a family member? Has the FBI been called in?" Neither Christy Sheldon's stoic expression nor her professional manner could hide the bubbly energy behind her questions.

Tara knew this case could be a career boost for the Channel 3 evening news reporter if she could break the story first. Christy would have to wait along with everyone else.

"We're not ruling anyone out at this time, but I can say we're turning our investigation away from the family right now. And yes, because of the type of case this is, we may be working closely with the FBI and other organizations."

A local newspaper reporter raised his voice over the other questions being thrown her way. "This is the third woman in two months who has come up missing and later found in a shallow grave here in Manhattan. Do you think we have another serial killer on the loose?"

Tara slowly nodded. "Yes. I believe we do."

* * *

Late Monday evening, an older man in his mid-fifties paced back and forth across the dirty, worn out linoleum of his living room, wringing his fat hands and occasionally plowing them through his few strands of greasy, gray hair. Every few seconds, he stopped and stared at the small television sitting on a wobbly stand. Then, he would pace some more. Stop and stare. And, pace. And, listen. And, whimper.

The evening news played over and over on the screen and in his mind as he switched channels from one station to another. Pausing on one channel, he heard the reporter say, "This is the third woman in two months who has come up missing and later found in a shallow grave. Detective Woods, do we have a serial killer on the loose?"

The woman answered. "Yes. I believe we do."

An explosive rage built up inside the older man. He wasn't fooled by the woman disguised as the detective on the news. He would know her anywhere. She was always trying to fool him, but he was smarter than she was.

Growling, he picked up the TV remote and threw it across the room, screaming out in a burning fury at the woman on the screen. "Mother, you stupid bitch. How many damn times do I have to kill you? How many?" Weakened from his misery, he slumped onto his broken-down couch. From the end table, he picked up an aged, faded picture of a once, youthful woman in her mid-twenties with shoulder-length black hair and a lustful grin. He cried out in mental anguish, "Mother, why? Why won't you stay dead?"

* * *

Early Tuesday morning, naked as a jaybird, Jake Taylor, Tara's often absent, live-in boyfriend spoon-fed her in bed. The last bite of delicious blueberry pancakes with homemade whipped topping he'd made while she was sleeping, melted in her mouth. Then, he kissed off the sweet, white dab of sweetness left on her lips.

She cupped his cheeks and gazed into his eyes. His hard, chiseled face with a sexy, ready smile, straight silky, black hair reaching his shoulders always stirred her senses. A toned, athletic body with a dark tan and his bedroom-blue eyes that seemed to look into her very soul was heart-stopping, yum yum, want-to-keep-him-naked gorgeous. She could spend hours gazing into his sensuous eyes as her playful hands roamed his beautiful body.

Tara scooted up further and deepened the kiss. His lips fed her hunger more than the delicious breakfast he'd cooked just for her, knowing she was exhausted.

Out of breath and shaking from need, she broke off the kiss and asked, "When will you be back?"

His hand glided up and down her curved waist and hip. "The antique art auction is Thursday and if I'm lucky enough to win the bid for the painting I'm after for my gallery, I'll be home by Saturday. Or sooner, if at all possible. I'm worried about this new case you're on and I hate leaving you alone."

She leaned forward for another kiss. "Don't worry. I'll be fine." The detective part of her hated the thought that he didn't think she could protect herself, but the woman in her felt safe and pampered.

Jake had been raised with three older sisters and a loving mother and father who'd taught him to treat women with a kind, protective heart and total respect. Two of the sisters were now married with kids and living within fifty miles of their parents in Philadelphia. The third sister, two years older than Jake lived in Baltimore and married to her nursing career.

The whole family and sometimes she herself when she wasn't on a case, met up once a month for one of his momma's home cooked meals, and Jake would catch a football game with his father, buddies and his brothers-in-laws. Seeing him with his family showed her what a good husband and father he would become some day. Hard not to love someone that wonderful and scrumptious, she thought.

"I'll always worry about you, because, I care about you. And, before you punch me for saying the 'worry' word, kiss me." He lowered his mouth to hers and his fingers teased her breast. Ending the kiss, he gazed into her eyes and winked. "I don't have to be at the airport for another two hours." He grinned and lifted himself until he was lying over her. "I can make the trip to the airport in twenty minutes. Less if we need longer."

CHAPTER TWO

Jake left around eight a.m. to catch his flight. An hour later, Tara sat behind her desk at the precinct drinking a bitter cup of black coffee from the vending machine and going over her notes on the latest murder when Dobbs entered her office munching on a donut and carrying a Styrofoam cup of coffee. A greasy, brown bag holding more donuts was clutched in one hand. He sat down across from her and pushed the bag across the desk. "Breakfast."

"No thanks. Jake cooked me pancakes this morning." She thought of what happened later and a grin appeared..

Dobbs pulled the donuts back to his side and humphed. "And, the man cooks, too. What does he not do?"

Tara shrugged and grinned. "Piss me off like my other partner?"

"That must be boring. Jake makes you a good housewife." He reached for another donut, stuffed part into his mouth and chewed.

Tara's brows narrowed. Before she could respond with an unlady like response, her phone rang. She pointed at Dobbs. "Believe me, Jake is all man and I was not bored this morning." She picked up her phone. "Detective Woods."

She sat straighter when Chief Haynes came on the line. "Grab Dobbs. I want you two in my office. Now."

"On our way, sir."

A moment later Tara and Dobbs entered their boss's office down the hall and sat across from him.

"What's up, Chief?" Dobbs asked.

Chief Haynes opened a dusty file marked 'COLD CASE'. "I thought about this case most of the night. Something kept nagging at me. Then, it hit me why it seemed so familiar." He tapped the manila folder and pushed it toward Tara and Dobbs. "Around thirty-two years ago your father and I worked on a very similar case. Three prostitutes around a seedier part of Manhattan were found dead in different locations, usually in wooded park areas. The way their bodies were positioned and decorated is very much like your case. But, he's getting more inventive. The victims we worked on were tied up with pink, lacy ribbon. Their hair was black, and they were all in their late twenties to early thirties, but what stuck in my mind was the doll lying in the victim's arms. It could be the same guy."

"If it is the same guy, it doesn't sound like he cares about their profession anymore. The latest victim sold real estate," Dobbs reminded them.

"True. But, the two before her worked the streets." Tara thumbed through the file. She glanced up in excitement. The heartwarming thought of working on a case her dad worked on was exhilarating, yet bittersweet. Her father should have been enjoying retirement, now. Instead, he and her mother had been murdered when she was only eight by a druggie needing money to buy more drugs.

Pushing the painful thought away, she concentrated on the old files in front of her. Any information they could gather for their own case would tip the odds to their favor. Glancing at the fading sheets of paper, her heart lurched when she recognized her father's handwriting. It was one of the small things from the 'before' time that she remembered. Along with her mother's perfume.

She glanced up at the man who had become her second father and mentored her after her dad's funeral. The expression in Chief Haynes eyes showed he recognized her pain, but he nodded, a signal for her to battle through it. She took a deep, breath and turned her thoughts back to the case. "Other than where the doll was placed on the body, both cases are very similar. You're right though, he's getting braver."

"Maybe it is the same guy," Dobbs added. "What happened with the case? This says it went cold."

The chief sighed and leaned back in his chair. "For the next two years four other prostitutes were murdered by who we thought was by the same guy.

We had several leads we were working on but, nothing panned out. Everyone we interviewed as suspects had credible alibis. No one else came forward with information. Back then, DNA testing was unavailable and we had no other evidence to break the case. Then, for the next thirty years, the murders just stopped." Haynes shrugged and leaned forward. "Until now."

Tara tapped the file with her finger. "So, was he having a thirty year cooling off period when his standard attacks were normally around a month or less? Or, did something else happen to stop his need to kill?"

Dobbs sighed. "I'd say the latter. I think all three of us are in agreement. Our guy is possibly the same person who killed thirty years, ago. We could argue that it's a copycat, but, from these files, any mention of the doll was also left out of any media reports back then, as well."

"Yeah, we left out that part. Copycats were as dominant back then, as now. We were able to eliminate that factor."

"Maybe a brainwashed son or daughter who witnessed the earlier murders and wanted to continue the family tradition to kill?" Tara wanted to dispel all possibilities in their case.

"Why would he or she wait thirty years to take up his father's mission?" Haynes asked. "But, you're right. We can't automatically assume this is a male. A female could easily overtake another woman. I agree with Cindy. The killer was probably mentally and/or physically abused by a family member and that's no specific gender prerequisite."

Tara nodded. "Except, Ben reported that our victims were raped. No sperm was found on any of them, but vaginal bruising confirmed the assaults. So, I'm leaning toward it being a male. Finding the reason he stopped killing might help solve our case. Are there any other old files we can look through? Working the cold case along with the new ones might be our best bet. Maybe if we re-interview everyone from back then, they might be more helpful now that time has passed."

"There were several boxes of material on the case. Check with our file clerk in the investigation room. She'll be able to help you. I'd start with one of our witnesses Maria Lopez if you can find her. She was a roommate of one of the victims. They both worked the streets together for protection. I always believed she was too frightened to tell us what she saw if, she saw anything at all. After thirty years, if she is still living, she may be more willing to talk." Haynes pointed toward the folder. "All of the main crucial information, the names of those we interviewed and the names of the officers involved in the case are in that file."

Tara stood. "Thanks Chief. We're on it."

* * *

At noon, Tara and Dobbs sat at her desk eating lunch and going over the names in the file the Chief had given them. They would pull the other files later.

They had one road block after another locating Maria Lopez. According to phone and court records, her last known address was a hundred and forty miles away, in Rhode Island. They were waiting on a phone call from the Providence PD confirming she still lived there before driving over two hours to question her.

Tara turned her attention to the possible suspects listed. So far, they'd discovered that two of the four had died within the past five years. "If it was one of the two still living, why did he just stop after three victims? What did he do for thirty years to get his rocks off?" she asked.

Dobbs took a bite off of his sandwich and swallowed. "Why did he start killing again? Hopefully, the DNA scrapings found under the fingernails of the early victims can help pinpoint our killer."

"That might be our only hope, but we can't wait for days until we get the results back." Tara tapped the file in front of her. "We know the two deceased suspects, Mark Tallent and Bob Seals didn't kill these last three victims. We can count them out for now. We need to concentrate on the other two, Jack Roberts and David Tyler."

Dobbs wiped his hands on his napkin and shook his head. "Tara, for years the Chief and your dad couldn't find anything on those two. I didn't know your dad, but I guarantee you the Chief wouldn't have left any stone unturned until he had solid proof against the killer. Even he had to admit their investigation was at a dead end. The men didn't run. They were just young boys in the wrong place at the wrong time. Nothing in the investigation proved anything other than they had been seen frequenting a neighborhood bar on the same street when and where two of the victims had been murdered. No crime in that."

Tara considered Dobbs' reasoning with reservation. "So, you think we're wasting our time checking out Roberts and Tyler? We both know most known serial killers hide among model citizens and most have a long cooling off period while they're finding other ways to feed their depraved cravings. A new woman in their life or a baby or even a playboy magazine subscription could satisfy them for awhile. How do we know they didn't grow bored with their life and needed a more satisfying stimulus and eventually returned to murder?"

"I don't think we need to completely rule them out. We need to talk to them, look into their past and make a decision about doing more, then. The Chief was right. People may be more willing to talk thirty years later. My money is on Lopez, too. She worked the streets in that area. She would've seen and heard everything going on around her, especially the well-known clients who liked to rough up the prostitutes. And, when three of her...colleagues come up missing, her eyes would've been peeled on anyone suspicious. I think she saw something, but was too scared to say anything."

Tara finished off her sandwich and threw the wrapping in a metal trashcan. "Sounds like a plan. If, we can find her. But we need to remember that our last victim wasn't a prostitute. She was a single woman with a legitimate career."

"Maybe he's refined his individual taste to classy ladies."

"Maybe. I don't buy it, though." She reached for the phone and called Officer Jackson. When he answered, she began. "Hey. This is Tara. Dobbs and I need you to dig further into Lori Crawford's life. See if she has secrets that her family isn't aware of or telling us about. If not, our killer has changed his targets. Also, we need to know what Jake Roberts and David Tyler have been up to all these years. Have Melinda help you. I'll send her the information we have." Melinda Cass was the precinct's be-bopping computer guru. If anyone could dig up any information on the computer for them, she could.

"I'm headed back to headquarters now. I'll let you know as soon as I find out anything."

"Thanks, Jackson. You always pull through for us."

Disconnecting, Tara turned her attention back to Dobbs. "The Chief's old files mention an Officer Boyd Brennan who helped work the case. He was their Jackson and did the footwork for them. He made detective and retired two years, ago. He might be able to shed more light than what's in these files."

"If he's still alive. We don't know how old he was thirty years ago. I'll ask the chief to help us locate him."

"Hopefully he was a young rookie back then and he and the Chief kept in touch." She glanced at her watch. Two hours had passed since they'd put in the call to the Providence police department requesting information about Lopez's whereabouts. Tara was too impatient to wait on phone calls. She redialed the number to the PD. "Yes. This is Detective Woods from Manhattan. I'd like to speak to Detective Shaw, please. Yes, I'll hold."

A moment later, Shaw came onto the line. "Detective Woods. I was getting ready to give you a call back."

"What do you have for us?"

"Not what you want to hear, but still good news. Maria Lopez's former landlady told us that Maria married a Felipe Martinez in 1998, and they moved to California two years later. The Department of Motor Vehicles was able to supply us with her latest address in Sacramento. I'm sending it as we speak."

She glanced at Dobbs. Her grin spread across her face. "Detective, you've been a big help. I owe you."

"No problem. Happy to help. I hope you find your guy and get the scumbag off of the streets."

"Planning on it, Detective."

Ending the call, she turned back to Dobbs. "Ever been to Sacramento?"

"Once or twice. I guess this means we need to make reservations for the next available flight out."

Tara nodded while bringing up her emails. "Yep. As soon as I print the address off, email the case information to Melinda for Jackson and we update the chief. Getting his boss's approval for the cost of our flight might take a lot of convincing."

* * *

Two hours later, after the chief's flight approval and speaking on the phone with Maria Martinez, who agreed to talk to them, Tara sat at her desk, relieved that things were falling into place. She ran her fingers through her hair and leaned back in her chair. At first,

Maria refused, saying she didn't want to rehash her past, which her husband knew nothing about. She finally relented when Tara promised they would meet with her while her husband was at work and assured her that they only wanted to ask her a few questions, nothing more. She would let Maria know when they would arrive.

Picking up her phone, she dialed the number to the JFK to make flight reservations. Five minutes later, she hung up. Her earlier relief had turned to frustration. All round-trip flights to Sacramento were fully booked up until 2:00 Wednesday afternoon. LaGuardia was even later.

Dobbs leaned back in his chair and stretched his long legs out in front of him. He rubbed his face, his annoyance evident. "We have no choice but to wait. I guess it's on to plan B, then. Since we can't leave until tomorrow and won't get back until Thursday after lunch some time, we still have plenty we need to do this evening."

Tara felt his frustration. Anytime they had a halt in their investigation it pushed them further behind in catching their killer. She nodded. "Right. First, I want to put together a crime board showing what we know and the timeline the chief and my Dad put together thirty years ago."

"Good idea. We can set up a past and present board and with any luck find a link other than how the bodies were positioned. I'll call and get the cold case files sent up. They may take awhile to go through."

"Yeah, that will work." Tara opened the manila folder the chief had given them earlier, while Dobbs called down to the file room. Then, she booted up her tablet and opened up her record database to read her notes on the latest victims.

An hour later, their board was organized by the victims, dates and locations. Pictures of the six deceased women were taped to the board along with Maria Lopez/Martinez and the pool of suspects, including the names of the four men investigated years before. Lines were drawn to connect the individual pictures from the past with a question mark beside each arrow.

She stepped back and stared at their work. Her heart skipped. She glanced at Dobbs. "Are you seeing what I'm seeing?"

Dobbs frowned. "I do, and it's freaking me out. All six women look enough alike to be sisters with their long, dark hair and hazel eyes. They're close to the same height, weight and age. If your hair was a shade darker, you'd look very much like them. I'm not liking this, Tara."

She didn't want to admit it, but the uncanny resemblance *was* eerie, so she changed the subject. Picking up the marker she wrote in bold letters beneath the pictures, 'MOTIVATION?' Below it, she listed,

1) 'Anger- Against Society?'
2) 'Rage- Perhaps abused as a child?'
3) 'Hostility toward dark haired women?'
4) 'Criminal?'
5) 'Money gain?'
6) 'Power/Thrill/Excitement?'
7) 'Psychosis-Hallucination-Paranoid- Mental?'

8) 'Sexual based- Sexual needs with victim?'

Then directly below that she wrote, 'AVAILABILITY-VULNERABILITY AND DESIREABILITY?'
1) 'Selects victim based upon the three listed above?'
2) 'Easy access to victim?'
3) 'Degree to which victim is susceptible to attack?'
4) 'The appeal and desire toward the victim?'

She returned the marker and turned to Dobbs. "Can you think of anything else?"

"I think that about covers it. We need to take this information to the daily briefing at four, which is ...," He glanced at his watch. "... in twenty minutes. Cindy should be there, as well. I'll give her a quick call to see if she's available to sit in."

"Good idea. She can give us a better profile and maybe add to or eliminate from our list."

* * *

An hour later, Tara and Dobbs left the meeting with the others with a small plan in place, at least more of one than they'd had before getting input from the others. Chief Haynes would contact retired officer, Detective Brennan. Melinda would search out more information about the two suspects from thirty years earlier and send the DNA from the older case to the lab for analysis. Jackson would question the family, friends and neighbors of Lori Crawford and Cindy would delve further into a possible profile. Tara and Dobbs would talk to Maria Martinez.

Walking back to her office, Tara stopped in the middle of the hallway and glanced at Dobbs. Worry etched between her brows. "How much time do you think we have before he kills, again?"

Dobbs sighed and ran his hand over his crew cut. "Not long. A few days at the most."

Her gut wrenched over the next victim's pain and demise if he wasn't caught in time. Long seconds passed before she nodded and continued on toward her office. "That's what I thought, too. We've got to catch this bastard, Dobbs."

His hand briefly touched her back. "We will."

Tara believed him. They'd never failed to solve a case before. She forced a smile. "Thanks. I don't want to look back years from now and have this as a cold case on my career profile. Join me for a beer later?"

"Hell, yeah. You're buying, right?"

"One. I'll buy you one for making me feel better about this case, then you're on your own."

Dobbs grinned. "I'll take what I can get from you."

"That's a good thing." She raised her chin and marched ahead of him, hiding her grin.

CHAPTER THREE

At nine o'clock Tuesday night, Tara slid onto the barstool next to Dobbs and ordered two beers. The 'Pig Sty' was the local bar where the cops hung out after work to unwind. Tonight, she needed to let the pissy day dissolve like a cloud from her mind.

She waved a hello across the darkened room to her working buddies from the precinct and turned back to Dobbs who was watching a game on the TV mounted on the wall. He thanked her for the beer and smiled. When he did, it seemed like every female in the bar swooned. Most women fell in lust with his sexy grin, combined with a deep dimple in his chin, blonde crew cut hair and emerald-green eyes.

The thirty-year old, six-foot-two-inch, two hundred pound, kickass, bad boy had been assigned her partner two years before. He was smart and dependable, the perfect partner for her. They worked well together, even though they constantly squabbled with a fun sexual undercurrent, with no serious meaning behind it. Tara acknowledged Dobbs was sexy and good looking. She wasn't blind to his charms, but he wasn't Jake.

She raised her voice to be heard over the TV hanging on the wall loudly broadcasting a football game. "Did you have any luck with the lead called in earlier?"

"No, it was another dead end just like the other thirty or so. Everyone is overly spooked with your announcement earlier of the possibility that a serial killer is still out there. Seems the noises the elderly landlady on Dogwood Street called about was her upstairs tenant and his woman having a little fun in the bedroom. How she came up with the bright idea their bed bangin' sounded like someone shoveling dirt in her backyard to bury someone is beyond me. Next time, you get to check out the crazies and I'll do the paperwork."

Tara burst out laughing and her mood lightened. "I'm sorry I missed it. Let me buy you another beer to make up for it."

"Ahh, I see what you're trying to do. You want to get me drunk so you can have your way with me?"

"In your dreams, pretty boy." She motioned for two more bottles of beer to be brought over and threw some money on the bar.

Dobbs laughed. "One of these days you're going to give in and let me show you how much of a man I am."

At ease with his innocent teasing and knowing Jake and Dobbs had a mutual liking and respect for each other, she couldn't resist a comeback. She grinned and winked. "Not as much of a man as Jake, my friend. I'm kind of biased when it comes to him. Maybe your women friends might appreciate your so-called manliness if you could keep them around long enough to get to know you."

"Ha, ha. Very funny." His attention turned to the bar's owner, Sandy, who sat the beers down in front of them.

Sandy brushed a strand of black hair from her face and glanced at Tara, her saucy grin widening. "Oh, I don't know, Tara. I figure he's extremely manly. Most women can't see it beneath all of that blown-up ego he wears as an armor. But, I can." She winked at him before walking over to a couple a few stools down.

His eyes lingered on her swaying hips as she moved on to other customers. His befuddled expression and goofy grin remained in place as he watched her pouring drinks.

Tara snapped her fingers to get his attention and laughed when he forced his gaze away from the owner and looked at her. Swallowing the last of her beer, she placed the bottle back on the counter and slid off the stool. "I'd say Sandy has your number. I'm turning in early. See you in the morning."

Dobbs drank the last of his beer and stood. "I'm not far behind you. Let me walk you to your car."

Tara waved him back to his seat. "Order yourself another beer, and this time talk to Sandy instead of drooling over her. I'll be fine."

He grinned. "I'm too cool to drool." He glanced toward Sandy, obviously torn between being a perfect gentleman by seeing to Tara's safety and a man wanting to flirt with a beautiful woman. "Are you sure?"

"Yes. I'm sure. Goodnight, Dobbs."

"Okay, stubborn. I'll stay a while longer. Be careful."

With a wry grin, she shook her head and left the bar. What was it with the men in her life always telling her to be careful? She was always careful and perfectly capable of taking care of herself. She had extensive training in combat and weaponry, for Pete's sake. Well, enough that Dobbs trusted her with his life whenever they went out on a call.

Tara reached her car with no mishaps. She'd intentionally parked in the most lighted area of the parking lot and near the front entrance. See? Careful. Except the light suddenly shattered into millions of pieces that fell onto the pavement along with a rock, leaving the area in complete darkness. Damn.

Feeling the hairs on the back of her neck rise, she glanced around the parking lot wishing she hadn't left her tactical flashlight and gun locked up in the car. They weren't allowed in the bar when officers were off duty. Keeping her eyes peeled, she used her remote to unlock the car door. The car beeped in the stillness and the headlights flashed giving her a brief view of the parking lot.

She heard a loud crunch of gravel behind her, and the nerves along her spine tingled. Tara swung around. A short, overweight man stood there, only a shadow in the moonlit darkness. Staring. His beady eyes were colorless, cold and empty. He took a step toward her.

Her eyes took in the empty parking lot. Damn, why hadn't she let Dobbs walk with her? She put her hand on the door handle and pulled until the door opened. "Look mister. I'm a detective. Do not come any closer. What do you want?"

His grin was evil. He took a step forward. Only inches from her, he reached into his pocket.

"Stop!" Tara yelled and side kicked out, her foot hitting him squarely in the chest. He staggered backwards, but never fell. Getting his balance, he came after her again. Her fist landed on his jaw, and her knee slammed into his stomach. He never flinched. He was a freakin' walking zombie.

Before she could back away and renew her attack, he grabbed her wrists, swung her around and pushed her flat up against the car.

"Hey! Hey you! Get your filthy hands off her."

She heard Dobbs' voice from behind her. His feet crunched on the gravel as he ran toward them. Suddenly, the man released her and shoved her to the ground. Quicker than a man his size should, he ran into the darkness, away from the parking lot and toward the line of stores on a street over.

She raised her head and called out. "I'm fine. Catch him. Go."

* * *

The expression in Dobbs' eyes hardened as he glanced toward the direction the man had ran. "Get in the car, lock the doors and call it in." He took off running toward his car to retrieve his gun and flashlight. Glancing back to make sure Tara had done as he'd ordered, he took off on foot after the bastard. The assailant had a huge head start. His car would be useless in following the creep if he hid inside any of the businesses lining the narrow streets.

Ten minutes later and two blocks down, Dobbs exited one of the buildings and spotted his man another block over, climbing into an older model sports car. Breathing heavily, Dobbs heard the motor roar to life and watched in anger and helplessness as the creep escaped.

Cursing, he made his way back to Tara. He heard sirens blaring in the distance and noticed the parking lot was full of the bar's customers and precinct officers who, minutes before, had been enjoying a beer and were now helping one of their own. He felt a good tingle in his gut when he noticed Sandy holding Tara's hand until the paramedics arrived. He would have to pursue that thought later.

CHAPTER FOUR

The paramedics cleaned the gravel and dirt out of Tara's hands and knees with a burning antiseptic before they began bandaging the cuts. She allowed it for a few minutes before swatting their hands away. She had too much to do to be fussed over. "I'm fine. Go find someone else to torture."

Without glancing their way, she moved off the ambulance bumper and made her way to Dobbs and Officer Jackson. She glanced up at Dobbs as Jackson, with a *you've-hurt-my-Tara-and-pissed-me-off* look, walk over to consult with the other officers on site. "Update me."

Dobbs glanced at her partially taped bandages and then back at the frustrated paramedics packing up.

Sandy was heading back into the bar. He shook his head and sighed at Tara's refusal to get treatment. "We don't have much to go on from your statement or what I saw. We've put out a BOLO on him and his vehicle. I got a partial license plate number, P 136 and Melinda is running those for us tonight. It may pan out for us and it might not. Jackson is having the security cameras around here checked out. The tapes might show us something. A team is scouring the parking lot looking for any evidence they can collect and bag."

Tara nodded, but, even with the team they depended on to do whatever was needed, Dobbs still looked preoccupied and worried. "And? I sense there's more on your mind. What are you not telling me?"

He shrugged, glanced at her and then away. "I don't know. Something doesn't seem right about this. We both saw him and have his vague description, but what's the motive? Attempted robbery is all I can come up with, but, my gut is telling me otherwise. He seemed more focused on you."

Tara shook her head and headed to her car. "No. I don't think it was robbery, either. He never demanded my money. He never said a single word to me. His eyes were crazed...like he wanted to kill me. Drugs, maybe?"

He started after her. "Possible. Except, he was lucid enough to make a fast getaway. It seemed to me he had a precise escape plan in place and knew exactly what he was doing, which worries me. Where do you think you're going?"

"Home." Her steps never slowed.

"Oh, no, you're not. You were just attacked, and we don't know why. The only part we can agree on is that he acted like he wanted to kill you. How do we know he doesn't know where you live? What if he tries to finish what he started? Manly Jake isn't there to protect you, remember?"

"Leave Jake out of this and don't you dare call him. He worries enough." She came to a stop, sighed and glanced at her watch. Almost midnight. "Look, Dobbs. I'm exhausted and need a good night's rest. We have a big case to solve and we both need to be focused for our trip tomorrow."

"Fine. But, I'm sleeping at your apartment until Jake comes home or that creep is caught." He held up his hand when she started to argue. "It's my way or I'm calling Jake. Your choice."

She glared at him and blew out a frustrated breath. "Okay. Okay. But only because I'm hurting and two seconds from conking out for the night. I do *not* want Jake bothered. Otherwise, you'd be in the hospital with your manliness wrapped in bandages after I showed you how much I appreciate you bossing me around."

He grinned, obviously enjoying her ill temper and thinking he'd won. "I'll follow you. And, you're welcome for saving your butt, tonight. Just give me a minute to talk to the crowd and we can leave."

Her fierce look was not a thank you. She gritted her teeth and climbed into her car.

A few minutes later, they left the bar parking lot after he assured the onlookers that the guy was long gone. Then he followed her to his apartment allowing him to pack a bag before she drove them back to her apartment.

CHAPTER FIVE

Tara would never admit it to Dobbs Wednesday morning, but knowing he was in the guest bedroom allowed her to sleep like a baby for the rest of the short night. That creep had freaked her out more than she'd liked. He'd caught her off guard and unarmed. Never again.

Dressed for work, and packed for their trip later, she grabbed the milk out of the fridge and placed it on the table next to the box of cereal and bowls. Pulling down two cups out of the cabinet, she poured the coffee and set it on the table. There. Breakfast was served.

She'd heard the shower stop a few minutes earlier and knew a hungry Dobbs would be stepping into her small kitchen at any time. It wouldn't be the first time he'd sat at her table, but spending the night was a different matter. Before the unsettling thought destroyed her composure, she sat and grabbed her coffee cup. She took a quick sip and scalded her tongue. "Damn, that was hot." The curse flew out of her mouth just as Dobbs walked into the kitchen.

"Well, thank you. If you think I look hot in these jeans wait until you see me in the ones I packed to take on the trip. Tight baby. Tight." With a bounce of his brows, he grinned, strutted around the kitchen table and sat in Jake's spot which she chose to ignore for the moment.

Tara sputtered. "I wasn't talking about you, smart butt. The coffee was hot, and I burned my tongue."

"Yeah, right. Whatever you say." He glanced at the cereal box and bowl sitting in front of him. "What? No pancakes or eggs and bacon for breakfast? Oh, that's right. Your man-wife does all the cooking, and he's gone."

"Eat your damn cereal and shut up." Her glare turned his teasing grin into a full-fledged laugh. She pointed her spoon at him. "I'll have you know I can cook when I want to."

"I believe you. I bet you can cook a mean TV dinner," he said, digging himself in further. He poured milk over his cereal and began to eat.

"Unless you want to wear that cereal, you'd better shut it, buster."

A twinkle appeared in his eyes. "I can't help it. You're so easy to tease. I'll tell you what, when we get back from Sacramento, I'll let you make me a home-cooked meal. Then, you can shove the fact that you can cook into my face. How does that sound?"

She stood and took her empty bowl to the sink. "You'll let me? I don't think so. But, you're on. I will willingly cook you a home-cooked meal. And, after you beg me for forgiveness for doubting my skills, I *will* make you pay for making fun of me. I'm fixing you up with a blind date for this weekend as payment."

"Oh no. Hell no. Uh uh. Not happening. I can find my own dates, thank you very much." His wide frightened gaze had her laughing out loud.

"Chicken."

"Hey, I believe I was plenty brave by volunteering to eat your cooking. Isn't that enough?"

Her brows narrowed. She held her laughter inside. She loved it when she had the upper hand with Dobbs. "No more negotiations. You've offended me and Jake. Unless you want me to tell him you called him a man-wife and insulted his girl, you need to make amends or face Jake. Do we have a deal?"

"You know Jake would agree with me, don't you?" Dobbs took a sip of his coffee.

"I'll call your mom."

He sighed, groaned and shook his head in defeat. "You fight dirty. One date?"

She nodded. "One meal?"

"Deal."

"Deal."

Oh hell. How was she going to learn how to cook a full meal before they got back from Sacramento?

* * *

At one p.m., their taxi parked in front of JFK so they could catch their two o'clock flight to Sacramento. If there were no delays or layovers, they would land in Sacramento five and a half hours later. With the difference in time zones, they'd arrive around four-thirty as planned and meet a very reluctant Maria Martinez's at a diner not far from her home. They would have only a brief hour to question Maria before she would have to rush away to beat her husband home. As a math teacher at the elementary school, her husband's normal routine very seldom varied.

* * *

The small, clean, family-owned diner showcasing home cooking was situated below an apartment and was sandwiched between a shoe store and a pharmacy. The bell on the door jingled as they entered. Glancing around the room with only a few customers at the tables, Tara immediately saw the person they were there to meet.

She studied the woman sitting in a corner booth. Maria Martinez looked older than her age of fifty-five. A life of prostitution during her early years had left its toll on her beauty. Her once wavy auburn hair had dramatically changed to straight black hair with gray strands peaking through the neat bun she now wore. The once slim and curvy figure had turned into a matronly plump body hidden beneath an inexpensive dress. The picture Tara and Dobbs carried with them for recognition was of a twenty-five-year old woman wearing a low-cut, short, red dress and a come-hither smile. Now, they saw an older woman with a worried tremble on her lips.

After introductions, they sat around the table. A young, uniformed waitress arrived to take their orders and returned moments later with their coffee.

Tara brought the white cup to her lips and blew on the hot liquid before savoring the taste of the rich, smooth coffee. She needed the caffeine boost after hours in flight. "Mrs. Martinez, thank you for meeting us."

Maria looked out the diner's window, her voice barely above a whisper. "I told the police everything I knew thirty years, ago." She shook her head and leaned toward them. "This is a bad idea. My husband can't find out about my sordid past. I've never told him. He's a good Christian man and would never understand, but, I know if he did know, he'd want me to help you. So, I'm willing to take the chance. I chose this diner because my husband and I have never been here before. No one should know me."

Tara laid a comforting hand on top of Maria's trembling hand. She understood. The woman's past was in the past and had no place in the present. "We understand and appreciate you talking to us. We'll do everything we can to keep you and your husband anonymous. Your statement should be all we need. We're just here for information. Thirty years ago, your roommate was a victim of a serial killer. Can you tell us anything about those past murders?"

Maria's shoulders rose and fell with a deep sigh. "You said on the phone that you believe the serial killer has returned."

Dobbs nodded with a compassionate glance. "Yes. We have evidence he's returned and resumed the murders, but now he's even more aggressive. He's braver and has upped his game. He's killed three times in the last two months."

Tara leaned forward. "Maria, we need your help to get this creep off the streets before he kills again. We think you knew something thirty years ago but were too afraid to speak up. You're safe now after all these years have passed and living across the country. Can you tell us what it is that you knew back then? We need to know everything. Even things you think aren't important could solve both cases."

Maria stared out the window. Her voice lowered and then she turned back and looked from Dobbs to Tara. "I think he was one of my johns."

CHAPTER SIX

Tara knew one important fact about prostitution and that was the 'johns' never told the girls their real name. She nodded for Maria to continue. "What name did he go by when he met with you? What can you tell us about him?"

Maria shifted in her chair. Her trembling fingers ran across her arms. "He said to call him 'Joe'. No last name. He looked like he was in his early twenties, maybe. An average looking guy with straight, black hair to his shoulders, slender build, a little shorter than me. I'm five-foot-eight. He pulled up to my corner in a late 1970's red Mustang and we went back to my apartment. Cheap hotels weren't my thing."

The waitress stopped by their table and freshened their coffee. When she walked off, Dobbs leaned forward. "What was it about the guy that made you suspicious?"

Her cheek color heightened, and she looked away, staring into space while her fingers shredded the napkin in her hand. Sucking in a deep breath, she glanced back at him. "I only saw him that one time, but I'll never forget. At first, he seemed nice. It didn't take me long to realize that boy was strange. His eyes were mean looking. That's the only way to describe them. Mean with the devil in them. He said I had to look young and innocent. He tied a pink ribbon in my hair and made me scrub off all my makeup. It wasn't enough for him. After awhile, he grew agitated. He couldn't perform and blamed me. He started screaming at me, saying I wasn't Mother. I got scared and told him to leave. He finally got dressed, and as he was leaving, a doll fell out of his jacket. He gave me a cold, I'll-kill-you stare, but instead of coming toward me as I feared, he picked up the doll and ran out of the room."

At the mention of the doll, Tara straightened. "What did the doll look like?"

"A fashion model type. Slender, with long, dark hair." She glanced down at the shredded napkin and then back at Tara and Dobbs. "It was the same doll the investigator said was found on my friend's body after she was murdered. She had black hair, too, you know?" Her lip quivered, a tear slid down her face and she whispered, "I think my dyed auburn hair saved my life."

* * *

At one, Thursday evening Tara and Dobbs' plane landed at JFK. By three o'clock they were in their daily briefing with Chief Haynes, Jackson, Cindy and Melinda, along with a couple of other officers. Tara and Dobbs filled them in on their visit with Maria.

Tara added, "We believe this 'Joe' is our man. Finding him will be a whole other monster. We know he targeted Maria's roommate Annie next after seeing her picture in their apartment. We believe he stalked her until he saw an opportunity to grab her. Maria is convinced the only reason he didn't kill her is because her hair was auburn at the time, not black like Annie's and the other two victims. So do I."

Chief Haynes leaned forward and glanced across the worn conference table. "Would she be able to identify him if we showed her a photo lineup? It wouldn't be admissible in court with her faded memory, but it could sure help us with the case."

Tara didn't want to raise anyone's hopes. "He'd look different after so long, but even so, she believes she'd recognize him if she saw him. Especially his 'demon' eyes as she called them. But this gets interesting. We showed her the pictures of the four suspects from the cold case. She told us without a doubt that her past statement still stands. None of them are our guy. She firmly believes this 'Joe' is who we need to be looking for in both cases."

"So, she wasn't lying back then when she swore she'd never seen those boys before," Jackson stated.

"No. And, she wouldn't have any reason to lie now. I think we can eliminate them from this case, too."

Cindy made notes in her tablet as they talked. "How did Maria say he was acting that night in her apartment? Was he acting strange? Overly talkative? Quiet? What was his behavior?" she asked.

Dobbs brushed the dust off his boot that rested across his left leg and answered, "She said he seemed gentle at first. Shy, quiet, a little self-conscious, maybe. She thought at the time that he'd never been with a woman before and spent about half an hour trying to bring him out of his shell enough to tell her what he wanted from her. He finally told her. Seems that his fantasies included her dressing like a young girl with pink ribbons in her hair. Then, when he couldn't perform, he grew hostile and agitated. Sadistic, even. He hurt her."

Cindy nodded and sat back in her chair. "I want to study this case a little longer and try to analyze his motive. If we can figure out his motive, we'll have a better chance capturing this guy. What's driving him to kill?" She looked around the room. Not waiting for an answer, she began. "Here are a few things we can look at. In all probability based on his patterns, he began as a petty criminal." She shrugged. "Maybe a Peeping Tom, sexual abuse or he tortured animals, or he could have been an arsonist. He would be highly anti-social with low self-esteem, no social graces, introverted and friendless. Maybe he begins imagining sexual scenarios and starts turning them into reality by acting out his visions. After a while, his imagination wasn't enough. He needed a stronger stimulus, like murder. After killing someone he'd relive it over and over for the gratification. Then, when the mental satisfaction began to fade he'd hunt another victim."

"What difference, if any, would there be from his younger, murdering years and now?" Tara asked.

Cindy clasped her hands on the tabletop and leaned forward. "After thirty years of controlling his urges, either by choice or circumstance, his behavior would've escalated, which it has. He's needing to act on the stimulus that's always inside him. It will never go away. He's needing to kill."

Tara nodded, letting the information Cindy gave sink in. "You're right. He's been controlling his urges for all these years. Do you have any theories as to why there's a long lull in his activities? Was he unable to carry them out for some reason?"

"It's possible he was incarcerated for something else," Dobbs offered.

"True. If he was involved in any of those crimes Cindy mentioned he might have a record on file." Tara glanced at Melinda. "Can you check out anyone being released in the last, say, four months who's served time for close to thirty years? It would be someone who lived in this area before and after his release."

Cindy held up one finger. "One other thing you might want to put into the equation. He mentioned to Maria about her not being his mother. With that, I feel confident saying he may have been abused mentally or sexually by his mother or a mother figure. That could be a strong motive for his murders. God knows we've seen it before."

Melinda made notes. "Sure. I'll check the Bureau's VICAP database, the Violent Criminal Apprehension Program. It helps determine the patterns or signatures the criminals does for satisfaction. Like leaving the doll behind or mother abuse, for instance. If there are any similar homicides in any other states, it will show up there and link together. If it's there, I should have you something by tomorrow."

Chief Haynes nodded and stood. "Great. Let us know what you find. Guys, good work. Let me know what manpower you'll need, and I'll get it approved. Anything else?"

"No, sir. That's all we have for now."

CHAPTER SEVEN

After the meeting, Tara had a rare free moment to take a break and Google the cooking channels. She knew both Jake and Dobbs loved Italian and didn't think she could go wrong with spaghetti. How hard could that be? She printed off a recipe from a chef she'd once watched on a cooking channel when she was bored. Shutting off her computer, she folded the paper and slipped it into her jeans' back pocket. She planned on leaving work early to shop for the ingredients she'd need.

First, she wanted to make sure Jake's flight would arrive on time. She dialed his number. "Hey sweetheart," she greeted when he answered. "Just checking in to see what time you'll be home."

"Hey babe. I just walked off the plane. I should be home in about an hour. Will you get off early?"

"Yes, I'm leaving in a few minutes to run by the grocery store. I thought I'd cook spaghetti tonight."

Silence.

Then, he cleared his throat. "Umm. Do you know how to cook spaghetti?"

"No, but I have a recipe."

Silence.

"Do I dare remind you that your kitchen skills are…shall I say, lacking? What brought this on?"

Tara sighed. He was right. She had a feeling this night was going to turn into a disaster unless she came clean and asked Jake for help. "Look, since Dobb's spent the night Tuesday, I offered him cereal for breakfast the next morning and that was a mistake."

"Wait. Dobbs spent the night? At our apartment?"

"Yep. I'll tell you all about it this evening after you get home. Anyway, he started teasing me about not knowing how to cook. By the time we got through arguing over who did all the cooking, me or you, we'd made a deal. If I fixed you and him a good dinner tonight, he'd agree to me setting him up with a blind date. So, that means we're having company tonight, and I'm making spaghetti."

Laughter came over the phone. "This I've got to see. Should be a fun evening. See you later, babe."

* * *

By five o'clock Tara was ready to pull her hair out. Standing in the grocery aisle, she glared at the variety of spaghetti packages and then back at the printed recipe in her hand. It didn't tell her what kind of spaghetti to buy. It just said spaghetti.

She pulled out her cell phone and dialed Jake. Less than a minute later, she hung up, smiling, and reached for the 'thin' kind that Jake recommended and liked.

Thirty minutes and several shopping bags later, she walked out of the grocery store pleased with herself. She'd only had to call Jake two more times before she'd gathered everything she needed.

Another twenty minutes and she was home. After unloading her grocery bags from her car's trunk, she carried them upstairs to her apartment. Suddenly, Tara sensed a creepy uneasiness in her gut. Glancing around, she didn't see anyone or anything. She shrugged off the eerie feeling, fumbled her keys out of her pocket and dropped them just outside her door. Before she could retrieve them, her door opened. Jake stood in the doorway with a sexy, welcoming smile.

"Here. Let me help you." In one sweep, he retrieved her keys then took the grocery bags out of her hands, following her into the kitchen.

She'd missed him. She waited until he placed the bags on the counter before she wrapped her arms around him and gave him a searing 'welcome home' kiss. He pulled her forward until their bodies met and deepened the kiss.

Someone cleared their throat, causing them to spring apart.

"Sorry if I'm interrupting." Dobbs stood in the kitchen entryway with a smirk on his face. "Carry on. I'm just going to my room."

"His room?" Jake looked down at her with a definite frown.

She patted his chest, stood on tiptoes and gave him a quick kiss. "I'll tell you later. Right now, I have spaghetti to cook."

"Oh no, you're not getting off the hook that easy. I want to know what's happened with this new case." His hands clenched his hips. He glanced at Dobbs. "I'm right, aren't I? You're here because you think she's in danger."

Dobbs nodded.

"Jake. Drop it." She hated being fussed over. She could take care of herself. Then, she thought of the incident in the parking lot and was thankful Dobbs showed up when she needed him.

"He has a right to know." Dobbs stood in the doorway with all joking put aside.

"Shut it, Dobbs." Her go-to-hell look should've muzzled him, but he ignored her.

"Tara was assaulted in the Pig Sty's parking lot Tuesday night."

"Why in the hell didn't someone call me?" Jake exploded.

"Because I was okay, Jake. There was no need worrying you." Her voice softened. She hated when her job caused him unnecessary worry, but she'd chosen the career she loved. No going back. No giving it up. Thankfully Jake was the type of man who didn't try to stop her from doing her job.

Jake cursed under his breath, but nodded before glancing back at Dobbs. "What else?"

"We don't know for sure if it was a random attack or if it has something to do with the homicide case we're working on."

While Tara unloaded the grocery bags, Dobbs filled Jake in on the latest serial killer case. When he got to the part of her attack in the parking lot, Jake's knuckles whitened as he clenched them into fists and cursed.

He glanced at Tara, his features softening. "Are you okay?"

She reached over and hugged him. "I'm fine. I promise."

He pulled her close and then reached over and shook Dobbs' hand. "Thanks, man. I can always trust you to look after her."

"Always."

She placed her hands on her hips. "Okay you two. I can very well look after myself. Now, if you're through being soppy babies, it's time to get cleaned up. I've got dinner to cook before our company arrives."

"Soppy babies?" Dobbs and Jake said in unison and looked at each other. Tara caught their rascally glance and took off running into the bathroom and locked the door before they had a chance to grab her. Their laughter followed her.

Her tension eased.

* * *

Thirty minutes later, after quick showers, the three met back up in the kitchen dressed in casual jeans and shirts.

Tara and Jake worked side by side in her small, modern kitchen with white cabinets and cream ceramic tile. As far as she was concerned, she could do without the new stainless-steel appliances and the double oven with a built-in grill. Before Jake had updated the kitchen the year before, a microwave and a hot plate were all she'd needed or wanted.

Glancing over at him, she smiled. She was more than a little pleased with herself. Between the recipe and Jake's helpful hints, she had the sauce simmering and the pasta cooking on the stove. Jake was tossing the salad and the garlic French bread was ready to stick into the oven to warm.

Dobbs, saying he didn't trust her, stayed in the kitchen to make sure she actually cooked the meal as she'd promised. As payback for his mistrust, she put him to work setting the table with her mother's china and silverware.

Her heart clenched when memories of watching her mother set their table flooded her senses, but she smiled. They were good memories.

"I don't think this blind date is going to show up. I think we should go ahead and eat. I'm hungry," Dobbs grumbled.

The hopeful look in his eyes made her laugh. She turned back to her sauce and gave it a stir. "Nope. She'll be here." The doorbell rang just as she finished her sentence. She gave Dobbs a told-you-so look before making her way to the front door.

Looking through the peephole, she saw their guest. Opening the door, she greeted her with a smile.

"Come on in. Just in time." She led the way to the kitchen. "Guys, Sandy is here."

Tara watched Dobbs' reaction. Bingo. He was taking in Sandy's shiny, black hair that fell straight down her back, her formfitting jeans and her blue blouse that enhanced her summer-sky-blue eyes. Oh yeah! His heated gaze told Tara he was pleased with what he saw.

"Hey, everyone. I brought wine," Sandy said, raising a bottle into the air. "It's the Pig Sty's best seller." Walking over to the guys, she gave Jake a brief hug and then glanced at Dobbs and smiled. "Don't look so shocked. You can close your mouth, now. Tara told me she didn't let you know I was your blind date." She leaned down and brushed his cheek with her lips.

Dobbs grinned taking in everything about the Pig Sty's owner whom he flirted with every chance he got. "Don't let it be said I can't follow orders." Wrapping an arm around her, his mouth did close. Over hers. He took his sweet time until Jake cleared his throat. Stepping back, he grinned not taking his eyes off of his blind date. "Hello, Sexy."

Sandy stepped back, smiling. "Hello yourself. I was beginning to think you'd never kiss me."

"Just biding my time, Sugar. But, now that I've started...," He threaded his thumbs through her belt loops and pulled her closer.

"Oh, good grief. Shall we leave you two alone?" Tara asked with her hands planted on her hips. Her words were flippant, but inside, she was high-fiving herself for pulling off both the meal and fixing

Dobb's up with the perfect date. Whether he liked it or not. And, it seemed he did.

* * *

The man followed the detective woman at a safe distance all the way from the precinct to the grocery store and then to her apartment building. Now he knew where the bitch lived.

After a thirty-minute vigilant watch from inside his vehicle, he saw the lady bar owner enter the detective's apartment building. He couldn't see which apartment she was going to, but he'd seen her talking to the detectives inside the bar and figured that's where she was headed. His interest rose. Black hair, tall, slim and a bad woman who worked in a bad place. She flirted with every man in there. She had no morals. Just like his mother. A whore. That's what she was. Scratching his crotch, he snickered and sat back to relax in his seat for the wait. She had to go home sometime. And, then he could start planning.

CHAPTER EIGHT

At eight Friday morning, Tara walked back into her office whistling a happy song. The dinner party the night before had turned out even better than she'd hoped. They'd had fun getting to know Sandy better in a quieter, non-work related atmosphere. She was funny, spirited and quick-witted, especially when bantering with Dobbs.

They'd learned she loved bartending, but what most of her regular customers didn't know was that she worked most nights to free up her days for taking Business Major courses at Manhattan College. Just three more months of payments to the bank and she would be the sole owner of the Pig Sty. She was already using her knowledge in business to cut costs and increase revenue by adding a kitchen with a new menu and new drinks at the bar that her customers loved.

At thirty years old, she was ready to slow her erratic life down. She was single and had never married or had children. Her parents and two brothers, who were both married with one son each, were her only family.

Work and school full time was a downer in her social life and energy. Her busy lifestyle was just as crazy as Dobbs', and she never knew when her plans might change because of her obligations. In Tara's opinion, Sandy was the perfect woman for Dobbs.

Except, Sandy chose to take a taxi home last night instead of letting Dobbs drive her home.

Tara got it. Sandy wasn't the type to jump feet first into a relationship. Tara didn't blame her. She'd been the same way when Jake had been brought into the precinct two years earlier on suspicion of art theft and murder. Claiming his innocence, he was released after the real culprit was captured within hours by Tara and Dobbs.

The sexual chemistry between Tara and Jake had begun at first sight during his interrogation. She'd ignored the strong feeling long after his innocence was proven. Even so, he'd pursued, and she'd run. It was two months later before he finally broke through all her self-applied barriers and she agreed to go out with him. She'd never regretted her decision. Never regretted asking him to move in with her.

Her career was important to her, and Jake's was just as important to him. Only, his wasn't as dangerous. It went against everything in her to put someone she cared about through intense worry while she was on a dangerous case. It was the same for her today. She hated worrying Jake, but he'd let her know early in their relationship that he would always be supportive of her career. And he had.

Sipping her black coffee, she smiled into the cup. Thank God, he hadn't given up on her in the beginning. And it helped that he was best friends with her partner, Dobbs. Life was good.

Her cell rang as she took another sip of coffee, breaking into her thoughts.

"Grab Dobbs. In my office in two." The line went dead before Tara could do more than recognize the chief's voice. Pushing the 'end' button she rose and headed across the hall. She stuck her head into Dobbs' office and saw him at his computer. "Hey, Chief wants us in his office. Now."

One of Dobbs' brows rose in question. Tara shrugged and they both rushed down the long hall to the chief's office. Tapping on the door, they entered. Officer Jackson stood with his shoulder leaned against the far wall. Melinda sat in one of the chairs across from Haynes.

"What's up, chief?" Tara and Dobbs sat in the two empty chairs beside Melinda and greeted everyone with a nod.

Chief Haynes sat back in his leather chair. Even at his size, the chair engulfed him. He glanced up at the officer. "Jackson, fill them in."

Nodding, Jackson straightened away from the wall and began. "The tire tracks we molded from the scene where Tara was attacked matches the tread of a late 1970's Mustang. I double checked with the manufacturer and they confirmed the molds showed they were not the originals but were probably purchased from a classic car catalogue who distributes the brand and size that matched the original tires. He gave me a list of companies off the internet who deal in them. If I can pin down the right company, I'm hoping they can give us a local name and address."

Tara's eyes widened with excitement. "Good job, Jackson. We need that name. Also, that's exactly how Maria described the car the perp drove thirty years, ago. A Late 1970's red Mustang."

Dobbs grinned. "Seems like he still has it, which means we can almost say for certain our serial killer tried to kill you. But, why?"

Chief Haynes rubbed the top of his head out of habit and spoke up. "I hate to think it, but it might've been because of the interview Tara gave Monday evening. He could've watched it and acted on his anger. *If*, it was him. There are probably hundreds of red 1976 Mustangs still around and drivable. We can't jump to conclusions."

Melinda spoke up. "I'm running the numbers now, Chief. Right now, I'm concentrating only on the surrounding boroughs where the murders have taken place. I'll span out if nothing hits. I should have something to report in a few hours."

"One thing we can eliminate for now is your research into the cold case suspects," Tara said. "The guy who attacked me is not Roberts or Tyler."

"Are you certain?"

"Positive, Chief. Unless he's had plastic surgery, changed his eye color and shrunk about a foot. My guy looks nothing like the photos."

"Great." Chief Haynes checked his watch. "I've got to rush to a meeting. Let me know as soon as you have something else. And, no more interviews for now. Let's keep this out of the media as much as we can."

"Yes, sir." The four filed out of the chief's office and headed to their own. A lot of work was ahead of them.

CHAPTER NINE

At ten a.m., Tara and Dobbs were working out in the basement gym at the police headquarters. Both had sweat dripping down their faces.

Using her gloved fists, she pounded the speed bag hanging from the ceiling, her feet stationary.

Laying on his back, Dobbs lifted heavy weights. Without glancing his way, Tara asked, "So, are you going to see Sandy, again?" The words puffed out between ragged breaths.

Dobbs blew out a lungful of air, lowered the weights to his chest and lifted. "Yeah. I'm taking her out for dinner tonight before she goes in for work."

Tara hid her smile, thinking again how perfect Sandy was for Dobbs. She was pretty, intelligent, successful and she didn't put up with his teasing bull crap. She could hold her own when it came to sassy mouths. They'd keep each other in line, whether they liked it or not.

"Why don't you and Jake join us?"

Tara pounded the bag. "Thanks, but you two need a chance to get to know each other without us around. Besides, Jake is teaching me how to bake tilapia with grilled vegetables tonight."

Dobbs glanced her way. "No way."

She nodded.

"You're taking this cooking thing seriously, aren't you?"

Tara stepped back. Taking the towel from around her neck, she swiped at the sweat running into her eyes. Shrugging, she nodded, a little embarrassed over wanting to learn. "Guess so. I missed having my mother teach me to cook when I was younger. But Jake is a wonderful substitute. It was fun cooking for you guys last night."

Dobbs raised the weights and set them on the resting bar. He sat up and swung his legs off the bench, heading for the showers. Suddenly, he stopped and turned back to her. "I'm sorry you missed out on your mom's lessons, but you have me and Jake, now. We're in no way a substitute, but we're the best you have." He offered her a cocky smile to lighten the mood. "The next chance we get some time off I'll show you how to master a mean grilled steak and baked potato. Now, that's a real man's meal."

One eyebrow rose involuntarily as she followed him to enter the women's showers, her heart contented with the people in her life. "Are you saying that Jake's tilapia isn't a real meal? Or, are you saying Jake isn't a real man?"

"Not to his face. With his muscles, he might beat the crap out of me. But, come on. Tilapia? If you're going to eat fish at least make it filleted fried catfish with fries and hushpuppies. Now, that's some good eating. I can taste it now."

Tara shuddered. "I gained five pounds and my arteries clogged just listening to you."

Dobbs just chuckled and entered the men's showers.

* * *

Thirty minutes later, Tara sat at her desk with Dobbs across from her, going over what they knew so far.

A sharp tap sounded on the door and Melinda walked in doing a happy dance. "Sorry to interrupt. Not really." She laughed. "'Cause you two are going to love me for this."

Dobbs grinned and stretched out his legs. "Spill it already. Quit being a tease."

Melinda stuck her tongue out at him, then turned toward Tara. "Considering over one hundred and eighty thousand Mustangs were sold in 1976 with a huge amount in New York alone, I've found five you might want to check out. Three of those five crashed in separate accidents and were turned into scrap metal not too many years after the cars were purchased. Another one is sitting in the family's garage. I talked to the wife of the man who owned that one, and she said her husband died about five years, ago, so he can't be linked to the latest murders. Their sixteen-year-old grandson is restoring the car. The last car I checked out really stands out more than the others. I got a super lead on the other guy, who bought a 1976 red Mustang fifty-five years ago from a local dealer in Manhattan. Unfortunately, the dealership closed down about ten years, ago."

Dobbs sat up straighter. "Damn. Is he still registering it?"

"Yep. And, the good news is his license plate number is YMP 136. Sound familiar."

Dobbs jumped to his feet and began pacing in front of the desk. "That's the same last letter and three numbers I saw on the car after Tara was attacked."

Tara shot a victory fist into the air. "Yesssss. Melinda, you're a genius. Please tell us you have a name to go along with the car."

"I was able to locate one of the salesmen who remembers selling the Mustang to a young local boy around that time. He remembered the boy's name because he'd gone to school with his daddy." Melinda checked her notes. "Um, the boy's name is Walt Landers, and his most recent address is in Kips Bay."

Tara glanced at Dobbs, unable to contain her excitement. "Melinda may have found our man. I say we drive out and have a little talk with him."

Dobbs nodded. "I'm with you. Melinda, will you check in with the chief and tell him what you've told us? Tell him we're headed to Landers' address." He raised a finger in the air. "One other thing. Ask the chief if this Landers guy was any part of their investigation from thirty years, ago. He might have a record on him already."

"You betcha. Good luck, guys."

Tara tossed her car keys to Dobbs. "Thanks Melinda. We owe you." She hurried her long strides to keep up with Dobbs' quick steps as they left the building. She was out of breath by the time they got to the car. Climbing in on the passenger side, she buckled her seatbelt and started programming the address into the GPS while Dobbs pulled away from the curb and headed Northeast on E 21st street toward 3rd Avenue.

Ten minutes later, they pulled up in front of the address Melinda had given them and parked. Tara glanced around at the older neighborhood lined with trashcans near the street. Quite. Not much traffic. Three young boys rode their bicycles past them on the sidewalk. The apartment building Landers lived in was a modest red brick, six story housing unit. An older couple sat on the steps leading to the front door, drinking coffee and enjoying the midmorning sun.

Climbing out of the car Tara glanced at the directions in her hand. Dobbs joined her on the sidewalk. "He's in apartment 410."

Greeting the couple on the steps, they walked past them and rang the buzzer to Landers' apartment and waited. Seconds later, they heard a deep male voice asking, "Who is it?"

Dobbs spoke into the intercom. "Detective Dobbs and Detective Woods. We need to speak to Walt Landers, if he's available."

"I'm Walt Landers. What's this all about?"

"We just need to ask you a few questions about a case we're working on. We're hoping you can help us."

"I don't know how I can help, but come on up." The buzzer rang and the door unlocked, giving them access into the building.

The door opened into a large family room for the tenants with a long sofa and several worn, but comfortable looking chairs, situated around the room. At the moment, no one was occupying them. Three end tables and one long table sat in the center of the room's ash-gray ceramic tile flooring. Several magazines and newspapers were scattered around. One side wall held the small mailboxes for each tenant. The elevator was located on the back wall, Tara observed.

Walking to the elevator, Dobbs pushed the 'up' button and the doors opened. Entering, he pressed the button to the fourth flour and the elevator began to inch upward. Finding apartment 410 was easy enough, and Dobbs knocked on the door.

A moment later, it opened and an older Caucasian male wearing a grungy, once white t-shirt, baggy shorts and knee socks motioned them inside.

Following Dobbs inside, she did a further assessment of the man. The man's dark, greasy hair was going bald on top. He was about four inches shorter than her 5' 8" and outweighed her by about fifty pounds. A slight body odor drifted across her nostrils. Tara's hopes were dashed. Landers' body size was similar to her attacker's, but, it wasn't him. The soft green eyes cleared him. She glanced toward Dobbs and shook her head. "Not him."

"You sure?"

She glanced back at Landers. He was watching them closely, clearly confused. "Positive. Unless he's wearing colored contact lens."

Her certainty didn't explain away the Mustang. She glanced around the apartment. She could see the living room and kitchen from where she stood. Three closed doors led into what she figured were two bedrooms and a bathroom. The old, worn Formica furniture had seen better days. Unwashed dishes sat in the sink. A musty smell blended with the food still left on the dishes caused her nose to curl slightly. Framed family photographs hung on the walls and newspapers cluttered the end tables.

"You said you wanted to ask me some questions. So ask. I'm a busy man and this is my day off." He didn't offer them a seat. Not that she would've sat on the filthy couch with the springs sticking through the top.

Tara glanced at Dobbs with a raised brow and then back to the guy. Pleasant fellow. "We'll make this quick, so we won't take up much more of your time. We understand you own a 1976 red Mustang."

"Yep, but I've never known that to be a crime."

"We have reason to believe it was used to leave the scene the other night when someone was attacked in the Pig Sty parking lot. The license plate number was seen by Detective Dobbs and it's the same as your vehicle's registered licensed number. We're also investigating a similar cold homicide where this same type of car was seen by a witness about thirty years ago and we believe recently. You know anything about that?"

He shook his head with a laugh. "No. It couldn't have been my car you saw. I've never been to the Pig Sty and my Mustang has been in storage for years. Last time I drove it was about three months, ago. You've got the wrong man and the wrong car."

"Maybe. Where were you this past Tuesday night between eight and nine?"

Landers rubbed his chin in thought. "I work swing shift at a convenience store nearby, so that night I was working the second shift from six to two." His flippant attitude seemed to change with her question. He was more forthcoming with information.

"Address of the store?"

After he gave her the address and she wrote it down, she asked. "What time did you go to dinner?"

"I always go at eight-thirty when I work that shift. I only get thirty minutes, so I always eat in the back room. Me and another worker take turns at dinner and breaks so the counter is never left unattended."

"Can this other employee vouch for you that night?"

He nodded his head. "Yes. The manager should have her latest address and phone number."

"Thanks," Dobbs said. "We'll check. In the meantime, do you mind if we take a look at your car in storage?"

Looking resigned, Landers nodded. "Yeah. Let me throw on some pants and I'll take you there."

Twenty minutes later, Dobbs pulled in behind Landers' Camry at the Kips Bay Storage. Landers buzzed open the mechanical metal gate, with his remote. The fence opened wide enough for their cars to drive through. They pulled their cars up in front of his shed and got out. Landers pulled out a key, but before he could use it, Dobbs stopped him, pointing at the bent metal around the key plate. He glanced at Tara. "Don't let him touch anything."

Dobbs went back to his car and pulled out three pairs of gloves and took them back to the building. He handed a pair to Tara and one to Landers. "Here, put these on, and don't touch anything." After putting on his own gloves, he opened the door, careful not to smear any fingerprints.

"Oh my God." The shocked comment came from Landers, who stood close behind him.

The storage room was empty.

CHAPTER TEN

Tara and Dobbs kept Landers on the premises long enough to answer their questions. According to him, his only family was his deceased father, one stepbrother, Ben Staffer, whom he'd lost touch with years ago, and one deceased stepsister, Patty Staffer. His stepbrother and a couple of his friends were the only ones who knew where the car was stored, and the last he'd heard, his stepbrother was still in the pen for murder. His friends knew they could borrow the car anytime they wanted, so there was no need to steal it. They also knew the car was his baby and would never ask. The only existing keys to the unit were the two he had on his keychain and the two the owner of the storage units kept in his office.

"What about the keys to your Mustang?" Dobbs asked.

"I have this one on my keychain and another hidden at my apartment. I haven't looked recently, but I'm sure it's still there."

Dobbs glanced his way. "Will you please look when you get home and let us know."

Landers nodded. "Sure. Okay."

With her hands on her hips, Tara stared at the empty storage unit and blew out a deep breath. She believed Landers was telling the truth. He was visibly shaken and angry. Or, maybe he was a damn good actor. No. He was being straight with them. Everything he'd told them could easily be confirmed, and he knew it. She turned back to him and mustered a weary smile. "You can go for now, Mr. Landers, but stay available. We may have more questions for you later."

"Don't worry. I'll be hounding you guys until my car is found. Until then, I guess I need to head to the police station to file a report." Getting into his car, he drove out of the parking lot, his tires squealing.

Tara called the crime lab, then she and Dobbs stopped by the storage units' office that was located inside a metal building. They needed to check a few things with the owner. The tall, gangly, older man with a slow drawl scratched his head and thought for a long minute. "Naw. I haven't seen anyone unusual around, and I don't have anyone on night shift duty, anymore. Can't afford 'em. No one from here would've seen anything within that three months span."

"What about security cameras? Could you show us the footage?"

The man shuffled his feet and looked down at the floor. "Um, …well, dang it. The camera in front went out on me around the first of the year. To be honest, I forgot all about it and I never got around to replacing it. I swear my memory has up and left me. I'll get it replaced this week."

Dobbs blew out a frustrated breath and asked. "Would you happen to have a list of all of your tenants, including any who've left in the last few months?"

"I sure do. I have to keep a spreadsheet, or I'd forget who owes me, you know? I'll print you off a copy."

A minute later, Dobbs moaned. He was reading down the list of eighteen names. He glanced up at the owner. "Who has the units on each side of Landers?"

The owner rubbed his jaw. "Let me see now. That would be Phillip Rodgers on the right side. He and his family downsized their home less than a year ago. Lot of their furniture and other stuff is stored inside. Then, on the left is Paul Jester. He owns a bakery off 24th Street. He keeps a lot of his catering supplies here for a quick pick up. Decent fellows. I don't think either of those guys would break in and steal a car. Both make a good living. They could buy their own car, you know?"

"What about your other tenants? Would you put any of them on the 'wouldn't put it past them to steal a car' list?" Dobbs asked.

Landers shook his head. "No. I can't think of anyone. I do background checks on all my tenants before they sign a lease. I've had some questionable ones here before, but they're long gone. These seem like pretty decent people. As long as they pay their rent on time and don't destroy my sheds, I have no problem with them."

"How many people have remotes for the gate?"

"I hand out two remotes to each unit." His eyes widened in sudden understanding. "Reckon someone stole one of the remotes? That's the only way they could've gotten past the fence."

Tara nodded. "It's possible. If you could contact your tenants for us and ask them if they still have both remotes we'd be grateful. Also, I'd appreciate it if you wouldn't mention to them what's going on. Just tell them you're doing a security check."

He puffed out his chest at being asked for a favor by the detectives. "I sure can. It may be a couple of days before I can get a hold of everyone, but I'll sure try."

Smiling, Tara reached into her pocket and dug out a card with her cell phone printed on it. She handed it to the owner. "That would be wonderful. Here's my number. Give me a call as soon as you find out something."

He beamed back at her, and a slight blush reddened his weathered cheeks. "My pleasure, Detective."

Leaving the office, Tara and Dobbs waited at Landers' unit until the crime guys arrived and secured the scene. Tara glanced at the black pavement surrounding the storage units without any hope. Impossible for any footprints to be found there. It was a long stretch that they would find any type of prints or DNA on the door. If they got lucky, they might find a footprint on the concrete floor inside.

The theft of the car could have happened anytime between three months ago and today. And, it had rained several days out of those spring and first of summer months that would've washed away any prints on the asphalt.

The morning was wasting away. They'd be better off spending their time looking for their killer. Tara poked Dobbs with her elbow. "Let's let them do their jobs and head back to the office. Maybe Melinda will have found something for us."

Dobbs nodded and shaded his eyes from the sun as he looked down the rows of buildings. He glanced back at Tara with a frown. "Yeah. Let's go. There's nothing else for us to do here until we hear back from forensics."

Thirty minutes later, they were sitting in Tara's office. Melinda had located a couple more local residents who owned late '70's Mustangs. She promised to let them know when she had the details worked out for them.

Now, Tara stared at the crime board they'd started three days before. She added Landers' name.

Dobbs tapped his pen on her desk, his forehead furrowed in thought. He stood and walked over to the board, staring at it as if it would tell him what he needed to know. After a while, he turned back to Tara. "You do know Landers could be lying through his teeth about not seeing his car for three months? He could've easily hidden it after this last murder, hoping to mislead us about the time span to throw us off track."

Tara followed his winding thoughts. "True. Or, we could be way off course."

"Okay. Let's list what we do know. One. We know the red Mustang I saw Tuesday night matches the description Maria gave us of the car from thirty years, ago. Two. We've already decided that the serial killer from the past and the present murders may be the same person. And, three, the person who attacked you is driving a car just like the one we're trying to locate. Four. You don't believe Landers is your attacker. If it isn't him, whoever it was had to realize that someone in the bar's parking lot got a good description of his car. He knew somebody was chasing him and more than likely got his license plate number. And, the number I saw just so happens to match the license plate number that's registered to him. Man, too much of a coincidence to me."

Tara sighed and twisted her upper body to loosen the kinks out of her back and shoulders, while her mind raced over what they were up against. "I know. I'm keeping an open mind until we check with Landers' boss after lunch. If he *was* at work and his co-workers can definitely say he was there the whole time, he'd have the perfect alibi. And if not, we'll bring him in and question him further."

She glanced at her watch. "It's lunch time, and we need a break. Let's run by and get a sandwich at the Bistro. By the time we get through eating, it should be time to meet the manager at the convenience store where Landers works. We'll know more, then."

"Sounds good to me. Wait!" Dobbs stopped inches from the door. "I just thought of something else."

"Let's make a quick stop by Melinda's office to see if she can find a picture of Landers in his late teens. Maybe in his yearbook or something. We can scan it and email it to Maria to see if she recognizes him as the one who she calls 'Joe'."

"Good idea. We'll need to call Maria to let her know it's coming, so she can view and delete the email before her husband gets home from work. We promised her we would be discreet." Tara stood and headed for the door.

Dobbs shook his head and followed. "We promised we'd *try* to be discreet. It depends on how the case goes."

"Well, we're going to try damn hard. The woman deserves to be happy for once in her life."

Dobbs laughed. "Sheath your claws, woman. I happen to agree with you."

"Well, hell. That's a first."

"And, the last."

CHAPTER ELEVEN

Two long hours later, Tara and Dobbs were no closer to finding their serial killer. The case of the missing Mustang had been turned over to the Auto Crime Division. Now they had time to delve further into Landers' present life.

Driving to the convenience store Landers had mentioned as his place of employment, they followed up on his statement about being at work when the murder had happened. His boss, a woman around her mid-thirties, told them that Landers was lazy and a slob, but he was dependable. He worked all shifts without a complaint and was always on time. She couldn't confirm that he'd been at work all of Tuesday night, but there was proof that he'd clocked in and out at the times he'd given them.

When Dobbs asked, she called his co-worker, Misty, who told them that yes, Landers had been there all night. She also confirmed that he'd taken his normal thirty-minute dinner break in the back room and was back at the counter by nine. He'd relieved her so she could take her break and she was back at nine-thirty. They ended their shift at two in the morning, just as he claimed.

Satisfied that Landers had spoken the truth, Tara followed Dobbs out of the convenience store. When they reached their car, she slid into the passenger seat, closing the door behind her. She ran her hands through her hair and glanced at Dobbs. "Now what?" she asked, reaching for her shades.

He started the car and put it in reverse, backing out of the small parking lot. His jaw was set hard. "Guess we start back at the beginning. Let's head back to headquarters. It's about time to update the chief."

***

During their Friday four o'clock briefing, Tara, Dobbs, Chief Haynes, Melinda, Jackson and Cindy sat around the table after the detective team from the three o'clock briefing filed out of the conference room.

Chief Haynes turned his full attention to them. "Give me the latest."

Tara and Dobbs told their group where they were at for the moment on the three murders. Nowhere. One small step forward and two large steps back. Tara closed her tablet. "We can't completely eliminate Landers. I don't want to take him off of the list, yet."

Chief Haynes rubbed his chin in thought before he spoke. "I remember this Landers guy from our cold case. He was a smart-ass punk kid. We investigated him but couldn't tie him to anything. He'd had a rough life growing up. He had a good-for-nothing father on his fourth marriage who pretty much left the boy to raise himself. If I remember right, the kid stayed in trouble with the law over crazy, petty things like stealing beer and cigarettes from a store, driving too fast and other things. His behavior is what gave him a solid alibi for the murders."

"How's that?" Dobbs asked.

"He was sitting in jail when one of the murders was committed. He was only a suspect at first because he was known to pick up a prostitute from that area on the weekends now and then."

Hanging on to every word, Tara's hope of having the right guy in their scope drained out of her. She sighed. "He seems to have a knack for having an alibi when one is needed. I guess we're back to where we started. That's all we have. Melinda, have you found anything else for us?"

Melinda shook her head. "Sorry. Not much. Do you know how many people in New York own 1970's Mustangs still have their cars registered? Hundreds. May I also tell you that most of them are red? It seems hopeless, but I've located one more person you might be interested in. He's not local, but close. Josh Mathews lives in a remote area in Harrison in Westchester County, a little over twenty miles northeast of here. He's in his early fifties, which would make him the right age for the cold cases. He spent the last fifteen years in the Clinton State Pen, and..." she checked her notes. "...was paroled back in January on good behavior."

"What was he in for?" Dobbs asked, making notes as she talked.

"Murder." She glanced up, offered a self-satisfied smile and figuratively let the mic drop. "Get this," she added. "He was convicted of killing his abusive mother. In the end, he pleaded guilty even though he said it was in self-defense."

Tara sipped her bottled water. Mathews sounded good, and would fit Cindy's profile, but she wasn't convinced. "You said he'd been incarcerated for the last fifteen years. What was he doing the fifteen years prior to that? Remember, our guy hasn't killed that we know of for the last thirty years, unless he changed his methods between then and now. And, if he did, why would he suddenly go back to his earlier MO? That doesn't make sense to me."

Cindy spoke up. "Good point, Tara. It's possible his methods changed, but unlikely. Most serial killers build and build on their style to achieve their ultimate desires, adding to them instead of doing less. And, don't forget the doll. He's leaving it behind for a reason. It meant something important to him thirty years, ago and it still means something to him today."

Dobbs nodded. "I agree with Cindy. Melinda, does your report say anything else about Mathew's past, like what was he doing prior to serving time?"

"Sorry guys. I didn't have time to check back further. I'll see what I can dig up for you."

The chief looked at his watch. "It's five o'clock. Tara and Dobbs, I'm with you on this. Mathews may or may not be our guy, but I still want him checked out in case our hunches are wrong. See if you can contact him and let me know what you find out."

"Will do, sir." At the Chief's dismissal, the five filed out of his office.

Fifteen minutes later, Tara disconnected her call to Mathews, who answered on the second ring. Unfortunately, he was in New Jersey visiting a cousin and wouldn't be home until Sunday evening. He agreed to drive straight from the airport to the station to meet with them at two.

Resigned to waiting, she glanced at Dobbs and filled him in. "There's not much more we can do for now. We may as well call it a day. What time are you picking up Sandy?"

"At seven. I made us a reservation at Le Bernardin."

"Oh, my. Fancy. You *are* trying to impress her. How did you get in so fast? Le Bernardin has a long waiting list."

He shrugged his broad shoulders, and an embarrassed crimson rose in his cheeks. "I was lucky enough to catch a last-minute cancellation when I called for a reservation."

"So, you begged the manager to move you ahead of everyone else?

"Something like that. I thought Sandy deserved a little fancy as hard as she's been working between classes and work."

Tara laughed, enjoying his discomfort. It was cute. "I can't argue with that. She'll love it. Why don't you go ahead and leave? We'll start again in the morning. I plan on heading out in a bit to spend some time with

Jake before he leaves out again on Saturday for an art auction."

"Sounds good to me. I'm taking Sandy back to the bar after dinner and hanging out there for awhile. You and Jake want to join us?"

Tara felt a blush burn her cheeks. "I don't think so. Remember, he's going to teach me how to bake Tilapia. We'll be a little occupied."

Dobbs laughed. "If Jake is half the man I think he is, he'll teach you more than baking, and I won't see you until in the morning."

Tara grinned like a schoolgirl. "I really hope so."

CHAPTER TWELVE

Her glossy, dark hair glimmered in the glow of the streetlights illuminating the shadowy neighborhood. Families enjoying their evening could be seen through the lower windows in their home. The smell of cigarette smoke and tequila drifted behind her. He swore he smelled her fear, as well. She repeatedly looked behind her, almost like she sensed him, swaying each time she did so from her drunken state.

She'd sensed his presence less than a block away and walked faster, her high heels tapping a fast drumbeat on the pavement. He was faster. His excitement soared. He loved the chase as much as he craved the kill.

Fevered excitement mingled with extreme disappointment. She wasn't his supreme kill…the one he really wanted, but he was smart enough to wait until the time was right. His perfect playmate wasn't going anywhere. He had plenty of time to work out every detail for the perfect evening with her. Or, longer. She would be worth the wait.

For now, he was willing to enjoy tonight's specimen. She wasn't as beautiful as the one he had picked out for the next time and nowhere near as breathtaking as his 'special' one, after that. The one he truly believed was the right one. Still this one would satisfy his needs until it was time for the others.

He weaved in and out of the alleys until he was close enough to reach out and touch her when she passed, but she wouldn't see him until it was too late.

He'd watched her for days. He knew her routine for every minute of every day. He knew what time she woke and what time she went to bed. He knew where she worked, what she had for breakfast and dinner and who she slept with on the weekends. Tonight, he'd spent the last hour watching her inside a nearby bar flirting and rubbing up against the men who were alone. Her slutty dress bared a large portion of her upper breasts and the hem barely reached past her butt cheeks. She let the men touch her, and in return they bought her drinks.

Sudden anger pumped through his veins. Whore. He slid from the darkness and his hand clamped over her mouth to stifle her screams. He drug her far into the alley. She was a fighter. Good. She struggled until the chloroform knocked her unconscious. Then, she was his.

"Mother's gonna die tonight."

CHAPTER THIRTEEN

By nine o'clock Friday evening, Tara sat across the dining table from Jake with a perfectly baked Tilapia and grilled vegetables on both of their plates. When she'd arrived home two hours earlier her quick shower had ended up taking a lot longer when Jake decided to join her.

Now, she took a sip of her wine and felt the stress of the day melt away. Then she took a bite of the fish and smiled across the table at Jake. "This is *so* good."

Jake's wink liquefied her bones. He poured more wine into her glass. "See? I told you it was easy. Cooking is a piece of cake once you've learned the basics. You're turning into a great cook."

Tara's smile widened at his compliment. "You're a great teacher. What else can you teach me?"

His smile reached his eyes. He leaned forward and crooked his index finger at her. "Come here," He whispered. When she did, he kissed her long and passionately. Leaning back, he asked, "How hungry are you?"

Coming off a high from his kiss, her voice came out as a croak. "Not very."

He stood and rounded the table. Taking her hand, he pulled her to her feet and led her toward the bedroom. "Let the lessons begin."

* * *

Tara's cell phone rang at five-forty-five Saturday morning. Pushing her hair away from her face, she reached for the phone on the bedside table, hoping the ringing hadn't awakened Jake. She cleared her voice. "Hello."

"We have another victim. Grab Dobbs and head to the lower end of Morningside Park. The coroner and lab are on their way."

Chief Haynes. Her gut churned and her head fell back on the pillow. Jake draped an arm across her stomach and pulled her toward him. "Yes, Sir. We'll be there as soon as possible." Her fingers hit the end button and she turned to Jake.

He leaned over and kissed her to comfort. "Another body?"

"Yeah. He's struck again."

"Babe, I'm sorry. I know you and Dobbs want to capture this creep more than anything. I wish I didn't have to leave you again."

"I'll be fine. Don't worry. I'll call you tonight." Swinging her legs off the side of the bed, she stood.

"I've got to call Dobbs and take a quick shower before he picks me up." She leaned over and kissed Jake, her lips wanting to linger. Regrettably, no time for that. "Have a safe trip and I'll see you Sunday night." She picked up her phone and headed toward the bathroom, her mind already focused on the latest murder.

* * *

Forty-five minutes later, Dobbs pulled into a parking spot outside Morningside Park and killed the motor. The light breeze was just strong enough to fan the ninety-degree temperature to bearable and set the leaves to swaying the leaves on the red oak trees lining the sidewalk. Dogs barked in the distance, mingling with the nearby traffic. Two joggers ran past them unaware of the murder scene just behind a few bushes on their left.

Walking a short distance, Tara and Dobbs rounded a corner. The coroner and forensic team were already on the scene.

Until given the okay, Tara and Dobbs stayed on the foot trail outside of the crime tape surrounding the possible evidence. From where they stood, Tara could see the body between the partially covered overgrown brush. It was resting in the same position as the other victims. A pink rose was placed between her fingers. She noticed the long, dark hair on the woman along with the familiar doll stuffed inside her.

Tara swallowed back the rising bile in her throat and turned to Dobbs. "She's pretty far back in those bushes, and it would've been just getting daylight when she was found. I'd like to know who found her and called it in and how he or she saw her in the first place."

She checked the local weather app on her phone. "The sun began rising around five-thirty and the chief called me at five-forty-five." She looked around the scene and shrugged. "I guess it's possible the body could've been seen from the jogging trail that early. Something seems off to me, though."

"Are you thinking the murderer might have called it in? Why would he change up his routine after successfully laying low for thirty years or more?"

"I don't know. Maybe he's older now and wants to be stopped. Or maybe we're being set up."

"Or, we have a copycat." Dobbs glanced up as Jackson rounded the corner. "Here's the person who can tell us."

Greeting Jackson, Tara filled him on her questions.

Jackson pushed back his hat and wiped away the sweat already beading on his brow. "It was an anonymous caller. A male who said he didn't want to get involved. The phone he used was untraceable. Probably a disposable. He claimed his dog started barking when they got near and it ran into the bushes. He tried to get him out and that's when he saw the body. There are a few bloody paw prints around the area to corroborate his story. I overheard one of the lab guys saying they thought the dog might have sniffed around, but didn't disturb anything other than the blood he stepped in. They can analyze that and eliminate those findings."

Tara rubbed her eyes and suppressed a yawn. "So much for my theories. But I still want to find this so-called jogger to see if he saw anything else. Jackson, can you help us locate this guy? Ask around. Most joggers have a routine they stick to every day. Surely, someone in the park that early in the morning is accustomed to seeing him run by at the same time every morning."

"Will do. Anything else?"

Tara glanced over at the coroner who had stood. "Not right now. I may have something else after I talk to Ben. Looks like he's wrapping up over there."

Dobbs began putting on his gloves before pulling out his booties and slipping into them. "Let's go talk to him."

Jackson left and they headed over to the taped off area. "Ben, what did you find?" Tara wanted a closer look at the body, but the forensic team was still gathering evidence inside the quarantined area.

The coroner pulled off his gloves and wiped his hands on a towel. He walked over to them. "This one was killed the same as the others. A .22 bullet between the eyes. Same pink ribbon around her wrists and the doll placed in the same area of her body. Black hair, early twenties. I think the autopsy will show she was killed elsewhere and dumped here earlier this morning. If I were a betting man, I'd say he killed her around midnight, let her bleed out, then left her here about four or five hours later."

Dobbs glanced over at the body. "I bet he took the time to get rid of any of his DNA on her. Her nails will be clean. No sperm. No fabrics. Nothing to tie back to him."

Ben nodded. "Visually, I didn't see anything. A swab will confirm if there's anything there. The forensic team is waiting until the body is removed before testing the ground beneath her for anything that might have fallen off her. Dirt, fabric or anything not consistent for this area."

Tara kicked at a clump of grass. Not finding this fiend wasn't an option for her. There had to be something or someone to point them to their killer before he killed, again.

She heard car doors slamming and saw the vans through the opening between the limbs. She glanced at Dobbs. "Let's get out of here. We're about to get swarmed by the media."

Dobbs looked toward the mob rushing around the corner of the bushes and cursed. "Too late, partner."

CHAPTER FOURTEEN

Escaping the media was impossible. The reporters were already out of their vans, and rushing toward them with their cameras and mics. Jackson managed to cut them off before they trampled any evidence or had a chance to view the latest fatality.

"Detective Woods. Detective Dobbs. Who's the victim?"

"Did the serial killer strike, again?"

"Are you any closer to finding this killer?"

The questions from different news reporters flew at them faster than the bullet taking the last victim's life. Tara held up her hand. "We've just arrived, guys. We don't know much more than you at this point. You know the rules. We have to ID the victim and notify the family. Chief Haynes will set up a media conference when we have something to tell."

"Oh, come on, Woods. Give us something to report." A young male reporter shoved his mic close to her face.

Tara stepped forward and pushed the mic away. "Come near me like that again and you'll be wearing handcuffs."

He backed up, but not before she noticed his embarrassment and the enraged glint in his eyes. Evidently, he had problems with female authority. Too bad.

Turning away from her, he motioned for his camera guy to move closer to the victim to take a picture.

Dobbs stepped in front of the camera man and stared him down. "Put your camera away, buddy or I'll charge you for obstruction of a crime scene investigation. Understand?" The camera man lowered his camera and backed up. Dobbs turned back to the reporters. "You heard Detective Woods. We have nothing for you. We'll give a statement when we do."

He stood with his hands on his hips until the reporters filed back to their vans with Jackson's forceful help. They grumbled and cursed all the way about not getting a story to take back to their bosses at the station. But, they had no choice.

Needing to lighten the tension around her, Tara said, "Oooooh, big, bad Dobbs frightened the media away. Sandy should've been here to see it. She would've been impressed." Teasing Dobbs had to be in her DNA. She loved it.

Dobbs flexed his biceps and smiled a naughty smile. "I have other admirable qualities that she will love even more."

Tara rolled her eyes. "Oh, good grief, lover boy. Pull your ego back a little."

"Hey, you had your chance with me. Too late, now." Dobbs headed back to the scene.

Tara shot back, determined to get in the last word. "Because I found something much better in Jake." Hurrying after him, she greeted Ben. "Can we come in, now?"

"Sure." Ben looked up from the victim for a moment and motioned them inside the crime tape. He nodded toward the girl. "This one isn't much different than the others. From the lesions and bruising, I would say she was raped more than once." He pointed at the girl's nails. "As I figured, they're as clean as a whistle. I don't have much hope in finding any semen, skin or fabric either. Or, common fragments to tell us where she was murdered." He shrugged. "I'll know more after the autopsy. We might luck out this time."

Tara studied the deceased girl and then glanced up at the medical examiner with a frown. "You said there's not much of a difference between the girls. What is different?"

Ben shuffled his feet as he gathered his thoughts. He glanced from the victim and back at Tara and Dobbs. "The time difference has changed. The bruising and cuts are fresh. No scabbing over. No fading bruises. He's not keeping them as long before killing them. Possibly just twenty-four hours instead of a week or longer."

Tara's heart skipped a beat. "Are you sure, Ben?"

"Yes, but, I'll let the autopsy back up my theory."

Was the killer becoming even more irrational or had his agenda abruptly changed? Tara studied the freshly mowed landscape around the vicious murder scene. Clumps of dirt disturbed the area where the body had been dragged to its resting place. She glanced back at Dobbs and Ben. "Why the rush? What has changed?"

Dobbs shrugged. "Without sounding rather callous, maybe she wasn't his type. Or, she fought him harder. It could be a number of things."

Ben shook his head. "Maybe, the last one? She's exactly the type he's been targeting. She endured the same type of cruelty as the other two and placed in the same position in her death. Like I said, the only thing I can tell that's changed is the length of time he's keeping them."

Tara trusted Ben's instincts and his medical knowledge. He'd never led them wrong. "I'll talk to Cindy. Maybe she can give us an idea on why he's stepping up his game. Can you pin down an approximate time of her capture and murder? That would give us a narrower window to work on."

"Yeah. I'll put a rush on the autopsy. I should have something for you by this evening. Hopefully, before we have another victim."

"Thanks Ben. Dobbs and I are heading out to see if we can find this girl's name and family. I'll ask Jackson to pull the surveillance footage for this area on our way out. Call me when you have something, okay?"

"You bet." Ben waved his hand in the air as a goodbye and turned away. He began gathering his tools and preparing to transport the body to the lab.

* * *

Tara and Dobbs hit the streets close to the murder scene. Along with other available police officers, they planned on canvassing the nearby area outwards toward Columbia University, Morningside Heights and further toward East Harlem. It was too early for the girls working the streets to make an appearance. She and Dobbs would show them the victim's picture later tonight. Hopefully, someone would talk.

A street over from the crime scene, Tara clamped her hands at her waist and looked at their surroundings. The nice neighborhood with medium income apartments wasn't luxurious, but all the residences looked homey and well taken care of. It was the type of place with friendly neighbors who would know each other, have block parties and barbeques. Young boys and girls rode bicycles on the sidewalks and played basketball and football in the courtyard. A few of the girls in pigtails and ponytails played on the steps with their dolls. It was a family neighborhood, very similar to what she'd enjoyed for the first eight years of her life. Her heart clenched as she added to her thoughts, "before her parents were murdered." She closed her eyes and took a deep breath to control her ache.

Dobbs moved next to her. "I think we need to move on. We've knocked on every door of these apartments. She's not from this area or someone would've recognized her picture. And, evidently, neither is the jogger. Let's check out the bars and businesses a block over. She has to buy groceries and eat out and have a social life of some kind."

"I agree. Plus, maybe someone from the University across the park might know something about her. If we can't find anyone who knows her, we can check back tonight after the girls begin working the streets, but I'm doubtful they'll talk. They'll be too scared of their john or too loyal to snitch on their own kind."

Dobbs headed back to the car, his steps heavy. "I know. The media and the mayor will be pressuring the chief to get this case solved quickly. We need to find something to throw to them like a bone to satisfy them for awhile. Anything to show them we're making a headway on this case."

Tara followed and slid into the passenger seat. Buckling up, she turned to her partner. "Then, let's go find it."

CHAPTER FIFTEEN

Eight o'clock Saturday night after not coming across anyone at any of the nearby shops or bars who knew the girl, Tara and Dobbs moved on.

An hour later, they approached the sixth working girl they'd seen since driving west on the seedier side of East Harlem. The other five hadn't been any help at all. Either they didn't know the victim, or they were lying through their teeth. Maybe they would luck out with this one. If not, they would move on to the next.

The young Caucasian girl with heavily applied make-up and highly teased bleached blonde hair leaned against the streetlamp, studying her long, red nails and looking bored until she looked up and tagged Tara and Dobbs as the police.

Her head jerked from side to side, looking from the street to the alley like she wanted to bolt somewhere.

Anywhere. She took another look at Tara and Dobbs and decided against it. Instead, with a resigned heave of breath she tugged down the hem of her short skirt and pulled the low-cut neck of her blouse up higher to cover her breasts. She shook her head and looked down at the sidewalk.

Muttering words that Tara didn't care to know, the girl straightened and faced them. "I'm so sick and tired of the law harassing me all the time. I ain't doing nothin' wrong."

Dobbs grinned. "Sure, you're not. You're just trying to get a breath of fresh air and enjoying the evening. And I'm Superman, out to save the world. Bullshit."

"Look. We're not here to bust you. At least not tonight. We need your help." Tara pulled the picture of the latest victim's upper body and face. It was very evident that she was deceased, but it was the only picture they had. "Have you seen this girl before?"

The girl glanced down at the picture. Her eyebrows widened. She swallowed hard and her hand flew to her red lips. "Angie?" The name tumbled out of her mouth. A sob escaped and she bent over at the waist hugging her stomach.

"Do you know her?" Tara's heart began to beat faster in excitement. Finally, they'd found someone who could identify their vic.

The girl's hand trembled. She straightened and reached for the picture for a better look. A few seconds later, she wiped the tears from her cheeks and nodded in certainty. "Yes. She's my roomie, Angie Shelton. She didn't come home last night, but I didn't think anything about it. She needed money and was always eager to earn a little cash. She was off last night, and went out partying with some friends. I just thought she'd hooked up with someone willing to pay." She looked from Tara to Dobbs, her eyes glistening with tears. "What happened?"

Dobbs softened his tone. "I'm sorry to inform you that your friend was murdered early this morning. Do you know of any family members we can contact who can come down to identify her?"

She shook her head. Her voice cracked. "She only has one older brother, and he lives in Kentucky. Their parents died in a car wreck about two years ago."

Tara stepped closer and put her hand on the girl's heaving shoulders. "What is your name?"

"You can call me Daisy."

"Thank you. Can you identify her for us to help with the case? The sooner we know positively that she's Angie, the sooner we can find the creep who killed her."

Daisy nodded. "Yes."

"Thank you. Would you be willing to go tonight? We can drive you and bring you back." Then Ben could start the final part of the autopsy.

The girl's shoulder's tensed and she looked around the area like she was expecting someone, probably her pimp. Then her shoulders relaxed, and she turned back to Tara. "Yeah. But I need to hurry back. I have someone meeting me later and he'll be pissed if I'm not here."

"We'll have you back in less than an hour. Will that work?"

"Yeah."

Dobbs brought the car around while Tara called Ben. Fifteen minutes later, they walked into the morgue's viewing room. The monitor was already turned on, displaying the room next door. They would be able to view the deceased and talk to Ben through the video camera connected to the screens.

Giving them a wave in greeting, Ben went over to the body lying on the examination table and lifted the sheet covering the victim's face.

The girl gasped and backed up a step. Then she nodded and turned away from the screen, her head bowed in grief. Between her sobs, she said, "That's Angie."

"Are you positive?"

Daisy nodded. "Yeah. I'm positive. Can we go now?" Without another word she rushed out of the room and ran toward the bathroom down the hall. Tara rushed after her and held the girl's hair back from her face as she lost everything in her stomach. When she was finished, Tara wet a paper towel and leaned against a wall, watching as the girl cleaned her face and rinsed out her mouth in the sink.

Leaning against a wall, Tara sympathized. She understood the desperation that forced girls into selling themselves. "I can find you help and the means to get off the streets. I don't have to tell you how dangerous it is to do the work you're doing."

The girl's eyes met Tara's in the mirror. Her spine stiffened. "Can you take me back now? I've done everything you've asked."

Tara sighed and pushed away from the wall. "Yeah. Let's go. Just remember I'm here for you and I can get you the help you need." With a curt nod from the girl, Tara led the way back to the car, hoping the girl would turn her life around, but, knowing she shouldn't hold her breath waiting for it to happen.

Dobbs met them at the morgue's exit door. Fifteen minutes later, the Daisy was back on the street. As they drove off, Tara turned to look back and froze. A young guy, most likely her pimp, approached her from the shadows. They began to argue and then he slapped her hard across the cheek.

"Stop the car!" Before Dobbs could come to a complete stop, Tara was out of the car and running back toward the guy. Dobbs threw the car into reverse and met Tara back at the street corner just as the pimp threw the girl onto the sidewalk and took off running. Gun drawn, Tara gave chase with Dobbs right behind her.

A block over they caught up with him. Dobbs wrestled him to the ground and handcuffed him while Tara read him his Miranda rights. The punk was no longer the boss, no longer in control and no longer brave when the police officer taking the call arrived. He still snarled liked an animal, and was still shouting out curses as Dobbs placed him in the back of the patrol car to be carried to the police station and booked.

"I own the bitch. I'll do what I want to her!"

Dobbs' smile turned lethal. "They'll take that into consideration back at the station, Bub. In the meantime, shut the hell up." He slammed the door and walked away.

Walking back to the car with Dobbs, Tara noticed Daisy was gone. Hopefully, she'd gone back to her family and left this life behind, but she doubted it.

She yawned and checked her watch. It was almost eleven o'clock. "I'll call the chief in the morning to update him. What do you say to calling it a night? I'm beat."

"Yeah, it's been a long day. I'll drop you off at your apartment. I plan on spending a few minutes with Sandy in the bar and then I'm headed home, myself. I'll check with you in the morning. When does Jake get back?"

"Tomorrow evening, and before you say anything, I'll be fine."

He *humphed*. "Your track record for getting in trouble tells me different."

"Look, you can walk me inside and then leave for your date. I'll lock up as soon as you leave, okay?" She climbed into the passenger seat.

Dobbs crawled behind the wheel and started the motor. "I'm not leaving until I know you're safe."

"Fine. But, you are leaving."

"Yes, then I'll leave, but only because Sandy will be waiting on me, and with your hair color you don't appear to be our creep's type of woman. Otherwise, you'd have me as a guest until Jake gets home."

Despite her weariness, Tara couldn't help feeling pleased Dobbs' feelings for Sandy were growing stronger every day. She couldn't have been happier for him. For once, she didn't tease him.

CHAPTER SIXTEEN

At eight o'clock Sunday morning after calling and filling in the chief on finding out their latest victim's identity, Tara made the dreaded call to Angie Shelton's brother to inform him of his sister's death. Through his grief, Jarrod Shelton told her he would be arriving in New York to take his baby sister back home to Kentucky for burial as soon as he could get a flight out. Understandably, he wanted answers on her murder. She was the only family he'd had left and now she was gone.

Before she disconnected the call, Tara gave him her cell phone number and asked him to call her as soon as he arrived. She needed to know everything about Angie's past and current life that might help her understand what led to her murder, and her brother was the person to ask. She didn't hold out much hope, though. The New York Angie was totally different than the Kentucky Angie her brother had known.

Tara rubbed her forehead and paced the kitchen. Making those kinds of calls never got any easier. Sighing, she reached for her cup and refilled it from the pot of freshly brewed coffee. She took it to the table and sat down, needing a few peaceful minutes to cleanse the cruel, dirty and murderous world out of her mind before she got dressed for church.

* * *

After church, Tara sat alone in a booth in her favorite diner enjoying a light chicken salad. Her job didn't allow her to attend church every Sunday, but she loved going when she had the chance. It was a routine her mother had ingrained in her at an early age. Thoughts of her family had been with her all morning, and the cold case her dad had worked on was keeping the memories fresh in her mind, lately. She'd needed the serenity of the morning service.

Normally, she didn't mind eating alone, but she missed the company and distraction today. Jake wouldn't get home until later that evening, and Dobbs was spending his day off with Sandy. Regrettably, those three, the chief, Jackson, Melinda, Cindy and a couple of neighbors were the only people she could call true friends. All the others were just acquaintances and co-workers.

How sad was that?

Everyone, like herself, was busy these days with no time to socialize. She twirled her tea glass on the diner's table, unconsciously smearing the water beneath it into a larger circle while she analyzed that disturbing thought.

Bull crap. Double bull crap. *Humph.* Her cleansing church thoughts were gone.

Trying to justify her lack of a social life failed horribly and sounded like a copout even to her. Other people managed to combined family life with a good social life. It was only she who had a problem making true friends. She knew she'd been using her parent's murder as a crutch for too many years to keep her heart to herself except for a very few people. Hell, she'd be twenty-nine in August. It was time for her to grow up and learn how to separate her demanding career from her other life. If Dobbs could do it, she could do it better. She grinned, feeling better after her inner pep talk.

When this case was over, she vowed she would talk to Jake about having a dinner party and inviting some of his colleagues, their neighbors and her friends from the precinct. He was an excellent cook, and she was learning. Maybe their guests could take turns hosting a dinner each week, or at least twice a month. It would be fun.

Then, she sighed, falling down to reality. It would be fun, but almost impossible. When this case was over, there would be another case and another and another. How could she laugh and party while someone lay dead in a morgue and a killer was on the loose? Still, she would talk to Jake. She knew he was tired of going to functions alone, even though he'd never complained. There *had* to be a way to have a fun, satisfying life and a career she loved without giving up one or the other. It had finally happened. She was getting to the age where she wanted it all.

But for now there was a killer on the loose.

Tara ate her salad without tasting it. Her mind became entirely focused on the case, enough, that she jumped when her phone rang.

"Listen," Dobbs began, without even a proper hello. "I'm going nuts sitting around. Sandy is in the shower getting ready for work and all I can think about is this case."

Tara grinned. She wasn't the only one who was obsessed with work. "Sooo, Sandy spent the night?"

"Nosey. I'm not feeding your sexual fantasies. You want to meet me at the precinct in a half an hour? I think we're overlooking something important, but for the life of me I can't figure it out. We need to regroup."

"I'm on my way."

* * *

Tara walked into Dobbs' office less than a half an hour later in one of the two church dresses she owned and a pair of black flats. She hadn't taken the time to go home and change.

He was sitting at his desk, rereading his notes on the case. He looked up when he heard her footsteps. She pointed toward her office. "Want to add our crime board to the equation?"

"Sure. Maybe something will pop out and hit us on the head. Right now, nothing is jumping out at me."

They walked over to her office, greeting a few officers who were unlucky to work the weekends.

One gave her a good-natured wolf whistle. They weren't used to seeing her in a dress. She grinned at him and winked. She glanced around the bullpen. Only a couple of criminals sat in the booking area. Looked like a slow workday for the precinct.

Dobbs sat in his usual chair in front of her desk while she stood in front of their crime board and added Angie Shelton's name and her picture.

She glanced at her watch. "We don't have much time. Josh Mathews, the other guy with a similar Mustang, will be here in less than an hour."

Dobbs leaned back in the chair and propped his sneaker clad feet on top of her desk. His fingertips steepled beneath his chin while he studied the board. "Right now, Mathews is our only hope," he said thoughtfully. "If he doesn't pan out, we're crap out of luck, but we need to check out every guy Melinda can come up with who owns that Mustang year model. I doubt if our victim's brother knew anything about his sister's illicit career or her so-called new friends in Manhattan. He won't be any help to us."

"I agree. I could tell from my phone conversation with Shelton that he knew nothing about his sister after she left home. I don't think they kept in touch. As far as Mathews, I still have concerns about the missing fifteen years before he went to the pen. It doesn't add up with the killer's MO. We know for certain there's been a thirty-year span between the three cold case killings involving the doll and our newest, similar murders with the doll, all inside the New York boroughs. If it is Mathews, what was he doing the other fifteen?"

Dobbs shrugged. "Living in another state, maybe? We can ask him, and we will, but I'd rather get the official information straight from Melinda if she can find out more. I'd also like to know if there are any connections between the latest victims other than their seedy careers. Did they know the same people? Did they hang out at the same places? Cold hard facts are what we need."

"True. I'll give Melinda a call."

Tara reached for the phone, but her hand stopped in midair when Jackson stuck his head in the doorway.

"Glad to see you guys are here. Got something for you. One of the officers who was part of the original investigation the chief and Detective Woods, I mean Detective Tara's dad were involved in is here to see both of you." He motioned for a man who looked like he was in his late sixties and had spent his career dealing with New York's worst scum of life into Tara's office. "This is Detective Boyd Brennan. He was Officer Brennan thirty years, ago when he was part of this case."

Tara felt her heart start pumping in excitement. Not only did the detective know information from the past investigation, which could be crucial to this case, but he'd known her dad.

He knew her dad.

CHAPTER SEVENTEEN

Detective Brennan shook their hands and Jackson returned to his office. "Haynes called me last night to let me know our cold case was reopened," Brennan said. "He knew I'd want to know and hoped I might remember some details about our investigations that he'd forgotten. He said I might find you here today, so I thought I'd stop by and offer my help if you need it."

"Believe me, we're grateful. We're no closer to solving this case than you were back then." Dobbs motioned toward the chair he'd vacated, offering it to Brennan, then went to his office and grabbed a straight back chair for himself.

While he was gone, Tara studied the ex-detective as he settled himself in the chair across from her desk.

She didn't recall ever meeting him during her childhood when her dad was alive or after she'd joined the police force. He didn't look like he'd let himself go after retirement. Even at his advanced age, his tall frame was erect, and buffed-up muscles were evident through his polo shirt. His salt-and-pepper hair was buzzed short, and she noted sharp intelligence and kindness in his piercing, blue eyes.

Brennan ran his long fingers along the crease in his khaki pant leg and sat back. He smiled at her "You remind me so much of your Dad in looks and mannerisms. Are you as stubborn, single-minded and determined as he was when working a case?"

She laughed. "Probably worse. He was my hero. I have so many questions to ask you about Dad, but now isn't the time. Maybe later?"

"Sure. He was my hero, too, and a good friend. I still miss the funny s.o.b.. Maybe we can have dinner later tonight and catch up?"

Tara forced the tears away. She didn't want him seeing what a wimp she could be over her Dad. Detectives were supposed to be too tough to cry. "I'd love to."

"Great. I'm looking forward to it." He waited until Dobbs sat before nodding toward the crime board. "If you don't mind, catch me up on these latest murders."

"I don't mind at all." All professionalism now, Tara walked to the board. Pointing at the three latest victim's photos, she began telling him every detail they knew about each one. After she was finished, she summed it up. "As you can see, I've added the cold case murders, hoping to link the past to the present. We know his targeted victims were easy picks. We believe he frequents the seedier locations at night when the women are standing on a street corner and he carefully chooses his next kill. He still prefers prostitutes with black hair, a slender build and in their twenties, even though our third victim, Lori Crawford, was a young mother with a four-year-old son who worked for a real estate agency. We're unsure why he deviated with her, except she looked so much like the others. As you can see from the pictures, he still has a thing for pink ribbons and dolls. The rose is a new touch, though. Cindy Tablor, our profiler, believes he has a 'mother' fixation."

Brennan rubbed his clean-shaven jaw in thought, stood and walked over to stand next to her to study the board closer. "A mother who hurt him. Hmm. Your Dad and I always believed it was a male doing the murders and your profiler's theory would fit in with someone who was lashing out in pain. I take it you agree with her conclusion?"

Tara nodded. "Yes. The ribbon and dolls threw us at first, but the autopsy showed no sign of injury from an instrument. Ben, our coroner, said the injuries were consistent to being raped by a male. The tears and cuts he noted were made from the doll being forcibly inserted. Maria Lopez, she's Maria Martinez now, told us she believes it was one of her male customers."

Brennan's sharp gaze rose to hers. "The same Maria Lopez we interviewed during our case? If I remember right, she was a roommate of one of the victims. We couldn't get her to talk. She was too scared."

"Yes. She's the one. She talked for us. Time and distance calmed her fears somewhat." Tara updated him about their interview with Maria and later, Walt Landers. She told him that two of the four suspects from the cold case were dead and about her own assault in the bar's parking lot a few days earlier.

"We showed Maria pictures of the other two living suspects from thirty years ago, and she claims neither one was her roommate's killer or her 'john'. We've put those two on the back burner for now."

Dobbs stood and joined them at the board. "We couldn't find anything on those four suspects, anyway. We decided they just happened to be at the wrong place at the right time, but, we haven't ruled them out completely. We may have to pull them in for questioning in the future, but for now we thought we should utilize our time elsewhere. Right now, we're following leads on '70s model red Mustangs. We saw in your original documents where a witness testified she saw a red Mustang the night of the cold case murders. Maria mentioned seeing a Mustang, and I saw a Mustang being driven away from the scene the night Tara was attacked."

"I remember the car mentioned. We searched for it, but never located the one we believed was used by the killer. We thought he might have disposed of it, at first. But, then it was seen, again. And, disappeared. We never located the Mustang."

"We're having the same problem. Our first suspect, Walt Landers, looked good for it but the Mustang he's had stored all this time was recently stolen. Our officers are trying to locate it."

"I remember Landers and his Mustang. We spent a great length of time checking into his background, and his whereabouts on the nights the girls were murdered."

"Chief Haynes said he had a solid alibi back then, too," Tara said.

Brennan nodded, his studied gaze still on the board. "He did. I remember. We had his car confiscated and tested. It was gone over with a fine-tooth comb. No blood, secretion or prints were found other than his and a couple of fresh prints from a friend who checked out, as well. Landers was a nut about keeping his red baby clean inside and out. If there was any other evidence, it was washed and wiped away before we took it."

"Do you remember anything about his family? From what we've learned, he had a rough childhood," Tara asked.

He rubbed his jaw. "If I remember right, he'd disowned any family he had and he hadn't seen them in years. His mother died in childbirth, so the 'mother' thing wouldn't fit his profile. His father was an asshole and a womanizer, 'scuse the language— who remarried and divorced several women, but he wasn't a murderer that we could prove. Plus, the father was too old to be our suspect. When we couldn't find anything on Walt Landers we ended up taking him off our list. What else do you have?"

Dobbs pointed to the picture of an older guy they had recently added to the board. "There's a second guy, Josh Mathews, who owns the same make, model and color. He should be here in a few minutes. You might want to sit in on the interview if you have time."

A spark of excitement appeared in his eyes. "I would. Thanks. Do you think he's our guy?"

"I'm not sure. He lives in Harrison in Westchester County, twenty miles northeast of here, which would be a long commute to haul bodies back and forth unless he has a place here in Manhattan he's using. He's in his early fifties and spent the last fifteen years in the Clinton State Pen. All twelve jurors unanimously found him guilty of the manslaughter of his own mother. An easy conviction. He was paroled back in January on good behavior."

Brennan's bushy eyebrows lifted. "Now, that's interesting to know. Abused, so he kills his mother and goes on a killing spree before getting caught?"

Tara glanced at the two men and frowned. Doubts resurfaced. "I'm still not convinced it could be him. As I mentioned to Dobbs earlier, one of the things I want to question him about is his where he was the fifteen years prior to being convicted."

Brennan nodded. "Good point. That would be a long time for inactivity. I'm anxious to see what he says." Glancing back at the board, he asked, "What else can you tell me about these women?"

Dobbs pointed to the last victim, Angie Shelton. "This is the fourth murder in a month. We believe the guy is changing his routine. Not only is he deviating from killing prostitutes, Ben noted that this girl's bruises and lesions were fresh. Angie's roommate saw her Friday night, and Ben placed her murder around midnight the same night. He thinks she was kept for just a few short hours instead of several days, like the others."

"Why? I wonder what's changed?"

Tara shrugged. "We don't know. Cindy thinks that his thirty-year abstinence has made him more aggressive, his needs more urgent. If that's the case, he may become careless and leave evidence behind. So far, he's left nothing for us to go on."

Brennan pinched his bottom lip in thought. "Our guy from the cold case was very careful before about not leaving any traces. If he's a convicted felon on record he'll be even more cautious."

"True," Tara said, "but even if he's not on record, we now have access to genetic genealogy testing. It uses non-victim DNA at a crime scene to connect it to the family members of a possible suspect. The tests could narrow down a lead to the suspect living in a close proximity to the victims or a possible connection to the girls."

"How accurate are these tests?"

"Accurate enough to solve a few cold cases that were dead in the water. We just have to find the DNA."

Brennan sat straighter. "I'm impressed."

Before Tara could add to the conversation, Jackson stuck his head in the doorway. "Sorry to interrupt, but our latest victim's brother just arrived."

"Great. Send him in." Dobbs pulled another chair into Tara's office and waited for Jackson to return with Jarrod Shelton.

"We're so sorry about your sister," Tara told him after everyone was settled and introductions had been made.

Shelton's head dropped. "Thank you."

Tara saw the resemblance between brother and sister. His swollen eyes proved he loved his baby sister no matter what she'd done in her limited lifetime.

"Can you tell us a little about Angie, why she chose to live the way she did on the streets?" Tara saw the exact instant Shelton saw his sister on the crime board. His hand went to his mouth, and he sucked in a sharp breath. Sobs wracked his body. She handed him a tissue and waited, letting him get his grief under control. They should have thought to take him to another room.

Moments later, he managed to respond. "Angie was the sweetest thing growing up. She was popular and athletic in school. Everyone loved her. It almost killed me and our parents when she ran away after she graduated. She'd had big plans to go to college to study architecture." Shelton chuckled through his tears. "Lord, the girl built her own playhouse in the back yard when she was only ten-years old. It was big enough for her to walk into and put her doll furniture all around. She loves building things." He glanced away. "Loved."

Tara's voice softened. "She sounds like someone who loved her family and friends and was happy with her life. Can you tell us what happened to change her plans?"

Jarrod Shelton's eyes hardened. "Drugs. A guy she'd dated all through high school got her hooked on cocaine and then dumped her right after they graduated. By then, she was playing with heroin. She had to have money to buy the drugs, so, she moved to Manhattan to make a lot of money the quickest way. Our parents hired a private investigator, and he found Angie three months, later. She was withdrawn and confrontational. She refused to come home, and they couldn't force her, but they tried.

"Mom and Dad were killed in a car wreck two years ago. Angie didn't come to the funerals and I haven't talked to her since. I knew something like this would happen to her. Damn it. I'm so pissed at her and hurting like hell. I just want to get her back home where she belongs." He broke down, sobbing uncontrollably.

Tara glanced at Dobbs and Brennan. Her heart broke for Jarrod. She walked around her desk and wrapped an arm around him with a promise. "We'll make sure it happens."

"Thank you. I appreciate it." He wiped his eyes and sniffled. "Guess I need to fill out whatever paperwork is needed and make a few phone calls to the funeral home, and then head back home. My flight back is later this evening." He stood, gave Tara a quick hug and shook Dobb's and Brennan's hands before leaving, looking like the burdens of the world were on his shoulder.

Tara sat down, near to tears. Jarrod had lost the only family he had left. She'd lived his pain.

Minutes later, Jackson returned. "Seems to be a busy day for a Sunday. Josh Mathews is here. He's in room number two."

Tara glanced at Dobbs and Brennan. "It's show time."

CHAPTER EIGHTEEN

Josh Mathews glanced up from his clenched hands when Tara and Dobbs entered the interrogation room. He sat straighter and attempted a smile that didn't reach his eyes. His gaze shifted from Dobbs to Tara.

He's nervous, Tara thought. Good. He was more apt to let the truth slip during their interview. If only they'd had time to find out more about him from Melinda. They'd have to wing it.

Tara sat in a straight-backed chair at the end of the stark, rectangular table and observed the man who looked to be in his early fifties. Dobbs sat beside her. A bottle of unopened water sat in front of Mathews.

He slowly unscrewed the cap off and took a drink. Watching. Waiting for them to make the first move.

Tara let him wait while she took in his prison tattoos, his short, bulky stature, and the expression in his eyes hardened that he couldn't completely hide. Though, he tried. His hair was thinning on top with silver strands running through the dark hair on the sides.

"Mr. Mathews, thank you for coming in. We appreciate your help. I'm Detective Woods and this is my partner Detective Dobbs. If you don't mind, we'd like to ask you a few questions."

Mathews shifted in his chair. "Nah. I don't mind. I never want to give anyone a reason to send me back to the pen, so that's why I'm here. I was told you're investigating a few murders and need my help. I'm not sure how me owning an older Mustang can help you find your killer, though."

She, as well as Dobbs, kept their expressions neutral.

A friendly 'good-ol'-boy-let's-have-a-drink-sometime-at-the-neighborhood-bar' expression stayed in place on Dobb's face. "We don't know that you can help us, but we have to check out every little thing. Women's lives are at stake. I hope you understand."

Mathews shrugged and relaxed a little. "Sure. I guess. What do you need to know?" He faced Dobbs and ignored Tara completely. A man to man thing. She seethed.

"Appreciate it, man." Dobbs reached into the folder lying on the table and slid the sheets of photographs down the table to Mathews. "Do you know any of these women?"

Mathews stared at the pictures and frowned. His Adam's apple moved up and down as he swallowed several times. He straightened his spine and snorted, his casual, friendly demeanor disappearing. Pushing the pictures back to Dobbs, he crossed his arms over his chest. "Do you think I'm stupid? You know I've been in prison for the last fifteen years. You've checked me out. Unless these women were in the same prison I was in, I don't know them. You're not gonna pin these murders on me."

"We're not trying to do that. Just trying to clear thing up. How long have you been out?" Tara asked.

Mathews shifted his hard gaze to Tara. "Six months."

"Then you've had plenty of time to get to know them." She stood and walked to Mathews' side. She placed her hands on the table and leaned in, no longer willing to play gender games with him. "Maybe you met them, stalked them and then killed them."

Mathews scooted his chair back so fast it fell to the floor. He stood and his fisted hands shot into the air and he lunged toward them. Tara and Dobbs pulled their weapons.

"Sit down," Dobbs ordered.

Mathews backed up and lowered his arms. His panicked gaze darted back and forth from her to Dobbs. He was no longer cocky, and his voice squeaked when he spoke. "Are you crazy, lady? Other than my mother, which the bitch well deserved, I've never killed anyone else."

Tara watched him trying to collect his emotions as she lowered her gun. "That would be Detective to you because I'm not feeling very lady-like right now. Talk to us."

Dobbs stood, glaring at their suspect. "You might want to answer her."

Mathews backed down. Then he picked up his chair from the floor and sat down. The look in his eyes is tortured. He glanced down at the table. "Look, I paid my dues. It's all in the court records. My mother use to beat me daily, starved me, kept me prisoner in my bedroom for years. When I was seventeen, I overpowered her and escaped. She tried to stop me, and I pushed her. She fell and hit her head hard on the bedpost. I didn't mean to kill her, but, I have to tell you, I was glad she was dead. I hated that woman."

He glanced up. "Read my report. You'll see I was captured in Missouri where I'd run after killing her. That's where the money I'd stolen from her ran out sixteen years later. I was thirty-three-years old when I was captured and brought back to New York to stand trial. I was on the run for sixteen years and I'd led an honest life until they used new technology to track my old DNA to my location. I've spent these last seventeen years in the courtroom and in prison."

His lifted his head in anger. Tears began to fall before he spoke. "Dammit. I've paid my dues." Wiping away the wetness, he brought himself under control and straightened. His gaze caught and held Tara's. "If you have any more questions, contact my lawyer. If that's all, I'd like to leave now."

Tara sighed and glanced at Dobbs. Looking back at Mathews, she nodded. "That's fine. We have no further questions for now. You can go." She was used to the suspects pulling the 'call my lawyer' bit, so she wasn't surprised. They had to let him go.

Dobbs stood and escorted Mathews from the room. A moment later, he returned and they joined Boyd Brennan in the viewing room next door. Brennan had heard and seen it all.

Tara spoke no one in particular, her voice little above a whisper. "I believe him." She glanced at Dobbs and Brennan wanting their thoughts. Was her gut wrong? Had she just released a serial killer, giving him another opportunity to kill again?

Dobbs leaned one shoulder against the wall next to the door. "I agree. Unless he's striving to be an award-winning actor, he's telling the truth, but I still want to read Melinda's full report on him before we take him off our list."

Brennan nodded. "I'm with you guys. My past experience has taught me not to stereotype anyone. Not all mother killers turn into serial killers, but you're right, Dobbs. You need to be cautious of Mathews until, you get the full report. I would keep him on my radar. Now, I think I'll get out of your hair and head home. Thank you both for letting me assist you in this case. It's very important for me to see this case to the end."

Tara smiled up at her late father's partner. "It was our pleasure. I was thinking, my boyfriend, Jake will be back from his trip late tonight. I know he would love to meet you. How about dinner tomorrow night? Dobbs, you and Sandy, too if you can make it. Maybe we can have a drink at the Pig Sty before we go to the restaurant."

Brennan smiled. "I'd love it. Around eight?"

"Eight is perfect."

"Sounds great. I'll see if Sandy can make it and get back with you," Dobbs told them.

Brennan dug into his pocket and withdrew a business card. "Here's my number. Call me later with directions. And, Tara, be prepared to tell me everything about yourself. I want to know if all of the wonderful things your Dad said about you are true."

Tara laughed, her heart swelling with happiness. "I think my father may have been a little biased where I'm concerned. I was a big daddy's girl. We'll have plenty of time to talk. I want to hear your story, too. I'm sorry to say that I was too young to remember meeting you back then."

"My pleasure and I remember you. You were such a beautiful, sweet child." Brennan said as they followed Dobbs out of the room.

Tara sighed as she watched Detective Brennan leave. She turned back to Dobbs and pointed a stern finger at him. "If you tell a living soul about how dang sappy I was a few minutes ago you'll be feeling my pointed shoe up your butt. Got it?"

Dobbs laughed, and wiggled his eyebrows. "Who? Me? Tell?"

"You're a dead man, Dobbs," Tara growled.

CHAPTER NINETEEN

Exhausted from a long day of combining Sunday worship and an even longer time at the office, Tara climbed the steps to her apartment. Jake wouldn't be home until around eight or so, depending on the traffic. That gave her three hours to shower, rest and attempt to put together a light meal of grilled chicken and vegetables for his homecoming. She had his cookbook with the easy recipes. What could go wrong?

Taking the last step, she turned the corner leading to her apartment door and pulled out her keys. A shadow moved, startling her. She reached into her purse for her gun, aimed it into the darkened corner and ordered, "Hold it right there. I'm with the NYPD and I have a gun."

The shadow stilled and she saw the outline of hands shooting into the air. "Whoa! Whoa! I'm unarmed. It's me, Walt Landers. I've been waiting on you for over an hour." He walked out into the light, his eyes never leaving the gun pointed at him.

Tara lowered her weapon, but kept her finger on the trigger. "Why?"

He shrugged and lowered his arms. "I just wanted to let you and Detective Dobbs know my Mustang was found in New Jersey, wrecked and abandoned. It was completely totaled. My baby is ruined."

He was a little overdramatic, and she hated drama. "I'm really sorry about your loss, but, more importantly, I want to know how you found my address." She itched to raise her gun and point it at his forehead. He'd taken her off guard and it pissed her off.

Again, he shrugged. "I Googled it."

Tara ground her teeth together. This was a freakin' scary world with freakin' scary people running around. "Well, don't do it again."

"Okay. Okay. Sorry. Can we get back to talking about my stolen car?" He wiggled his work khakis up over his large belly and continued, "I'm going out of my way to help you with your murder case by letting you know whoever stole and wrecked my car might be your man and he might be in New Jersey." He took a deep breath. "I thought you'd be more enthusiastic than this. And, more appreciative for that matter."

Tara sighed, her deep exhaustion weighing heavily on her. She ran her fingers through her hair, her thoughts spinning. He was right. It needed to be checked out. "Look. I do appreciate it and I promise I'll look into it. Can you give me the name of the person who informed you about your car?"

"Yep. It was Detective Paul Banks of the NJPD. After I mourned my baby's demise, I told him you might be calling him. You are, aren't you?"

"Yes. I will."

"And you'll let me know what you find out? I want the bastard who stole my Mustang to pay."

"I guess you have the right to know. I'll try my best to find the thief, but I can't promise anything."

He stuck his hand out to shake. "Your word is all I need. Thanks. You know how to find me when you find out anything?"

Tara's lip curved up at the corners. "Yep. Even without Google, I can find you. Thank you for your help, Mr. Landers."

An embarrassed grin materialized. "You're welcome." He pointed toward the stairs. "Um…I'll be going now. Oh, wait. I meant to tell you, I have both sets of my car keys."

She frowned. "Is there anyone who had access to them, who might have had an extra key made?"

"A lot of people have been in and out of my home, but I don't know of anyone who'd go to the trouble to steal the key, have an extra made and then return it. Well, maybe one person, but he hasn't been to my apartment in years. He's the type I wouldn't leave alone for one second, anyway. Never trusted the guy."

"Who would that be?" Tara asked, her interest suddenly piqued.

"My stepbrother, Ben Staffer. He's been in the pen for thirty years, though, so it couldn't be him."

His time release would be easy to confirm, Tara thought. "Let us know if you think of anyone else."

"Will do. I'll be thinking on it."

Tara watched him go and turned toward her apartment. Unlocking the door, she stepped inside and threw the keys onto the foyer table. Then, she took her phone out of her purse and dialed Dobbs. Her well planned evening had just been blown to hell.

* * *

Detective Paul Banks of the Auto Crime Division seemed to dislike being bothered on a Sunday evening to discuss an out-of-state stolen car case. Tough. He shouldn't have given the dispatcher his cell phone number to give out.

With a little pressure from Tara and an attitude one level up from rudeness—he agreed to email her the investigation report asap. Other than that, he insisted she call back the next day if she needed anything else from him. So much for loyalty amongst detectives.

Twenty-five minutes later, Tara and Dobbs sat at her kitchen table pouring over the pages of the emailed reports along with pictures of the crime scene she'd printed off. Banks might be an overbearing A-hole, but at least he was thorough and professional. The car had been found dangling over a high-level wooded cliff. A large pine tree kept it from falling several yards to the rocky bottom. A passerby happened to notice the sun's glint off the back bumper and called it in.

The car was empty, and there was no body found in the surrounding area. No one had called in an accident or missing person report. The driver had simply disappeared.

And, the car was in neutral.

"It says here that the car has been taken to the NJPD containment garage for their forensic team to go over for evidence." Tara sighed. "Tomorrow."

Dobbs scooted back his chair and stretched out his legs. Exhaustion showed around his eyes. "It looks like we're at a dead end for now. First thing in the morning I want to contact the owner of the storage building where Landers kept the Mustang. I'm hoping he contacted his renters for us. I would be very interested to know if everyone still has both of their gate remotes, since there's no way anyone can enter without one."

"Unless the gate didn't properly shut behind the last person leaving. Anyone could stick something on the moving rail to keep it from closing all the way. Half an inch would be enough. Wait until night and slip back, push the gate open and steal the car."

Dobbs ran a hand over his head. "Sounds plausible. We know from Landers and the storage owner that all the keys to the unit were accounted for and someone gained entry by forcing the storage door's key mechanism plate loose. No key was needed to enter his unit.

"Right, but, that doesn't explain how the car was taken without a car key."

"Hotwired, most likely. Or, it could've been trailered out with the intention of replacing the ignition switch and wiring later. Whoever stole it, were either professionals who were in and out within minutes, or they knew about the cameras not working and the length of the police patrol routine to calculate them the time they needed. The storage units aren't located on a main street and wouldn't have much car traffic late at night for them to worry about."

Tara nodded. "That makes sense. You said 'they'. You think there's more than one person involved?"

Dobbs shrugged. "It would be tricky and time consuming for one person to do it, but it's possible. That is, if we believe Landers and it *was* stolen."

"That's the kicker. I don't know what to believe. Even a sleezeball can be honest sometime."

With her mind racing, Tara rose and grabbed them both a beer from the fridge. She placed one in front of Dobbs and sat back down. She raised her opened bottle to her partner in a silent toast, took a drink and set her bottle on the table. "So, assuming Landers is telling the truth, why would anyone go to that much trouble to steal a car, take it to New Jersey and intentionally wreck it? The car was in neutral, so it had to be intentional. Why?"

Dobbs took a swallow of his beer and gave her a glib grin. "To get rid of the evidence, of course. I guarantee you the perp intended the car to hit the bottom of the cliff in a blazing ball of fire. They weren't expecting the pine tree to stop its momentum, and they didn't stick around to watch."

Tara grinned and raised her bottle in the air to click against his. "How fortunate for us if their plans were foiled."

Dobbs finished his beer and stood. "Don't celebrate just yet. We don't actually know whether the stolen Mustang has anything to do with our homicide cases or not. It could just be a coincidence. Either way, there's nothing else we can do tonight."

He glanced at his watch and headed for the door. "I have just over an hour before I need to meet Sandy at her apartment. We have a dinner reservation for eight o'clock. You and Jake want to come?"

"Nope. We're staying in tonight. I'm going to cook him a homemade meal."

Dobbs choked back a laugh. "Tell Jake to call me if I need to take him to the emergency room."

Tara growled deep in her throat, and raised her bottle, aiming it at his head. "If you don't get out of here it's going to be you needing the emergency room, buster."

The door shut behind him and she heard his laughter as he climbed down the steps. She grinned and shook her head. She'd get him back.

CHAPTER TWENTY

At eight-fifteen, Tara welcomed Jake home with a warm kiss and a home-cooked meal. The kiss was perfect, but the meal was sadly lacking in doneness. She blamed it on Landers for messing with her time.

But, to hers and Jake's deep gratification she was able to properly welcome him home in a most satisfying way in the bedroom for the next half hour while the chicken finished cooking on the grill. Short, but perfect, blissful timing.

Looking up from her plate, at peace inside for a change, she watched Jake slice into his perfectly cooked chicken. The juices ran onto his plate. Perfect. Next, he took a bite of the tender, grilled zucchini and squash. His eyes closed as he moaned. "This is so good. You did wonderful, babe. I'm so proud of you."

Staring across the table at him, her eyes teared and her wounded heart knew this was a man to hold onto for life. It was hard for her to admit it to herself, much less to him, that he was her world, that she needed him and couldn't fathom ever losing him. As sappy as it sounded, he was her soul mate.

Still, it was so hard to say the words to him even though he told her often how much he cared for her, so, she didn't. He was always careful not to say the 'love' word knowing she'd run away in panic. They were both tiptoeing around discussing their growing relationship. She knew it hurt him and scared her.

Maybe it was meeting her dad's partner and friend today that had her emotions all out of whack. Maybe she was tired of feeling like a half of a person. Maybe she was sick of being afraid of having a permanent relationship. Or, maybe it was all of the above. She wanted it all. Jake and her career. Before she realized what was happening, she blurted out, "I love you."

And, wished she could take it back.

Until she saw the stunned expression on his face.

Jake's fork stilled halfway to his lips. Then dropped to the plate.

Her heart did funny somersaults.

His eyes searched hers. "That's the first time you've told me. You can't take it back now."

"Maybe I need to."

"Nope." Her eyes widened in surprise and pleasure as he stood, made it to her side, lifted her into his arms and carried her to their bedroom. He made sure she was speechless for the next hour.

Later, lying drowsy in his arms, he whispered against her skin. "You don't know how happy you've made me. Did you mean it?"

Tara sighed and snuggled against him. She chose her words carefully. "Yes. I meant it, but, hear me out. It doesn't change anything. I can't give up my career. I'm sorry. And I can't throw away what we have together, either. You know how dangerous my job can be whenever I'm working a case. To be brutally honest, I could be killed tomorrow, and then where would you be? If anything happened to me it would hurt you so much less if you *didn't* love me. I thought I could have both. But, I don't know if that's even possible."

Jake raised onto his elbow and stared down at her. She saw a flicker of frustration in his eyes. "Have I ever asked you to give up your career?"

Dammit. He had her there. "No."

His eyes turned tender, his voice low and intense. "No. And I never will. I love you. If I can't stop it, you sure can't, so I guess we'll both have to get over it. I'm a grown man. I can make up my own mind about my feelings for you. You can push me away as much as you want to, but I will keep coming back. Every. Time. Got it?"

She got it and believed it. That didn't mean she agreed. She tried explaining one more time. "I can't guarantee we'll have a future together. You know the hell I've gone through after losing my parents. I would never put someone I love through that same hell. You know that."

But she was by loving him.

He simply lay back down, his head on one end of her pillow and said, "Whatever time we have is worth it, babe." He squeezed her tight and fell asleep almost instantly, exhaustion and jet lag overtaking him.

She smiled and whispered, "I do love you, you big goon."

* * *

At 10:00 p.m. Tara was still unable to sleep. Untangling herself from Jake's side, she tiptoed into the kitchen where she began putting away the food and cleaning the kitchen. When it was spotless, she refilled her wine glass and sat down at the table, her mind filled with memories and dreams about her future, hopefully with Jake. Was it possible for her to be a tough detective at work and still have a life of docile domestic bliss at home? Well, strike the docile part. Docile wasn't in her DNA. But she'd proven to herself this week that she could feed and take care of Jake. Other women juggled both a career and family life and they were happy. She had a lot to learn, but she could do it. Even if she only had a short life to give him. *Hey, we might live to be rocking chair lovers reaching the ripe old age of a hundred or more. Who knows?*

She sighed, realizing she hadn't told him about her meeting with Brennan or their dinner date tomorrow night. Nor, had she asked him about his trip. She swirled her wine glass on the table. *I've been putting Jake second place to my cases. I don't deserve him, and he deserves a life more normal than what I can give him. What was I thinking by blurting out the 'Love' word to him?"*

She laid her forehead on the table and panicked at the enormity of what those three little words meant. "Dammit," she thought. I can't risk letting my heart take over my thinking, or, the next thing I know I'll be wanting a home, white picket fence, kids and a dog. That's insane." "Oh, Chief Haynes. I'm sorry, but I can't investigate the murder today. Baby Livia has a fever and I can't leave her until she's feeling better," she mimicked sarcastically.

Yeah, right. That would fly high with the Chief while women were being murdered in his city. Unwanted tears slid down her face. She drained her glass and placed it in the dishwasher and returned to bed. She curled up against Jake, her heart being tugged in two different directions. Listening to the gentle breathing of her friend and lover next to her soothed her and made her want. Want Jake. Want a family. Want his love. "Baby steps, Tara," she told herself. "You're a strong woman. Conquer one obstacle at a time and you might just find the happiness you want. Need. Without destroying Jake."

But a gun pointed at her by a killer didn't scare her as much as the total commitment and responsibility that came with loving someone. Then again, she'd always loved the name, Livia."

* * *

At six Monday morning, Jake brought her breakfast in bed, wearing only his briefs and a sultry smile. She glanced down at the scrambled eggs, bacon and coffee... blessed coffee.

She scooted up in the bed and took the tray. "Thank you. This looks delicious." She patted the bed beside her. "Join me?"

"My pleasure." He sat on the side of the bed and scooted over next to her, reaching over to steal a slice of bacon. Taking a bite, he pointed the rest of the meat toward her. Without missing a beat he continued their conversation from the previous night. "Don't get me wrong. I'm happy as hell that you finally admitted you love me, but I'm a little curious as to why you decided to blurt it out last night. I know you well enough to know something happened to give you that extra push to voice it. Mind telling me the reason?"

Tara swallowed a sip of coffee and placed the cup back onto the tray. She offered him a wide, sultry smile and licked her lips, hoping he'd take the bait and let her distract him. "I'd rather you kissed me and make me late for work."

He grinned. "Not going to happen, babe. You're not going to sidetrack me."

She grinned back at him and began eating her breakfast, knowing he was on to her stall tactics. "I'd rather hear about your trip first."

"It was a great trip. I was able to purchase the paintings I wanted for the gallery. Now, it's your turn."

Glancing his way, she sighed and finished her coffee. "It's a long story."

"We have time." He adjusted his pillow, settled back against the headrest and crossed his arms over his chest.

He wasn't going anywhere, she thought. Most of the time she found his stubbornness endearing, but not this morning, when it was aimed at her. She leaned over and placed the tray on the bedside table before moving back to lie beside him. Quietly at first, she began telling him about the latest murder and where they were on the investigation. Then, she told him about her dad's partner and friend stopping by headquarters to help with the investigation. "I hope you don't mind, but I told Brennan we'd meet him this evening at Sandy's bar and then go on to dinner to do a little reminiscing about my parents. Dobbs and Sandy might come, too."

"Babe, that's wonderful. Of course, I don't mind. I'd love to know more about your parents, too. You know everything about my crazy family, but I know very little about yours."

Tara shrugged and realized, "I don't know much about them myself. I only know them as my parents, and what family and friends have told me after they were murdered. Brennan was with my father day after day for years. Other than my mom, he and Chief Haynes probably knew Dad better than anyone. Speaking of the chief, I know he'll want to come, too. I'll ask him as soon as I get in this morning."

Jake smiled. "Sounds good. Still want to be late for work?"

She grinned, slid under the covers and wrapped an arm around his neck. "Yeah, but, it's not going to happen. Got to catch a serial killer." She kissed him once more before jumping out of bed and heading for the shower.

CHAPTER TWENTY-ONE

Tara walked into her office a little out of breath. It was only eight a.m., but she was running late, even though she'd rushed to work while talking to Dobbs on the phone all the way in. A new, disturbing thought kept nagging at her during the drive. It was such a crazy thought that she kept it to herself. Or, was it?

Her mind kept going back to the Mustang. She and Dobbs had known since speaking with Maria Martinez that the car was involved in the thirty year old murders. And, they knew it was involved in the current cases as well.

What if the killer had stolen Landers' car, driven to New Jersey hours away and gone on a killing spree? One of many? What if this wasn't the first time the

Mustang had been stolen, used as an easy mode of transportation for murders in another state and then taken back to the storage unit with no one the wiser? Just wiped his hands clean and walked away. How many other states and murders could he be involved in that they knew nothing about?

Then again, why leave his familiar hunting ground in New York? It was a big state. There was plenty of local prey without having to travel.

Another question. Did the killer somehow know they were investigating the vehicle and decide to get rid of the evidence? Did he have another means of transportation? Something plain to fly beneath their radar? Something unnoticeable?

Maybe they had it all wrong. The stolen car may not have any relation to their case. Just a coincidence. Or, it could blow their case wide open if they were lucky. Tara hoped so.

She still had so many questions with no answers.

Dobbs came into her office carrying two Styrofoam cups of coffee from the vending machine. Pushing one across the table, he greeted her and took his usual chair across from her. "I just got off the phone with the owner of the storage units where Landers' car was stolen. The owner checked with all the renters, and they all confirmed they still had both gate remotes. Another dead end."

"If they're telling the truth."

"True. He believes they are but asked them to stop by with them as soon as possible to make sure they do. I've also asked Melinda and Jackson to meet with us this morning to go over a few of the things we talked about on the way in this morning. They should be here any minute."

"Good. Maybe talking it out with them will help." Tara took a sip of her coffee and grimaced. "I've got to bring my own coffee pot down here. This is disgusting, but better than nothing."

"Do you even know how to make coffee?"

She aimed a murderous look at him but missed her chance to retaliate when Melinda and Jackson entered her office. "Hey guys. Have a seat. Dobbs and I have a few questions that you two might be able to help us answer."

Jackson and Melinda took the two extra chairs. "We'll help where we can," Jackson said. "I have a few updates for you when you're ready."

"Great. We want to hear them before you leave." Tara leaned back in her chair and began by telling them about her thoughts and questions from earlier that morning. "To me, the biggest puzzle is why would someone drive two hours into another state to get rid of the car? There are plenty of secluded spots just minutes away from the storage unit."

Dobbs pinched his bottom lip, his gaze focused on the crime board. He shrugged. "Maybe to throw us off? But, how would he know we were checking out that particular Mustang?"

"He may have heard Landers or someone from the storage unit talking about it. Or, who knows? It could've been Landers himself. He's a weird, suspicious dude, anyway. I'm not ruling him out, completely. I could be way off, though. It could've been a random thief who stole the car, got wind that we were checking out Landers' Mustang, got scared and decided to get rid of it. We could even be dealing with a crime ring with a chop shop," Tara added, knowing they needed to examine every angle.

Jackson didn't look convinced. "He's working on his own. The job was too amateurish. If it was an organized crime ring, they would've, as you said, had a chop shop to cut it down or simply repainted, given it new papers and a license plate to do a quick black market resell. This guy didn't have the equipment or place to do anything other than wreck the car. Fortunately for us, his plan didn't work as well as he'd expected."

Tara sighed, rubbed her face and glanced at her team, her gaze resting on Dobbs. "Jackson's right. We have to go at this thinking it's only one person involved."

"Our murderer. I agree. I think our best option is to confirm any and all leads. Melinda, we need you to check out the New Jersey criminal database. See if there are any murders that are similar to our guy's M.O. or the Mustang's history."

Melinda took notes and nodded. "Will do. I've looked into our database list of U.S. homicide cases that are similar to ours. I'd figured that a female victim with a doll would be easy to locate on the database, but, nothing has popped up so far. I'll concentrate on New Jersey. Maybe it hasn't been updated, yet."

"Thanks, Melinda. I think from what you just said, we can safely say he's stayed in New York, unless he recently decided to hit New Jersey on a whim."

Dobbs turned to Jackson. "You can stay on top of matching the prints found inside the wrecked Mustang. Let us know as soon as NJPD releases the crime report."

"On it." Jackson stood, prepared to leave.

"Hold up." Tara raised her hand. "You were going to give us an update before you left."

"Guess I'm getting old and forgetful." Jackson grinned and sat back down. "Sadly, I don't have any good news. The officers assigned to me have been knocking on doors, viewing camera footage and walking the streets for two days. No one admits to seeing anything at the time of any of the murders. The jogger who found Shelton checked out. His own security camera was his witness. He never left home during the known timeframe. It showed him and his wife having drinks on their patio until almost midnight and then they went inside. Their vehicles never left during the night."

"And, of course, they were each other's alibis," Tara added.

"Correct. We have nothing. Nada. I hate to admit it, but this guy's smart and has a plan. He knows when to hit. He knew no one would be around on the streets at that time of night. I mean, this is New York, for God's sake. There are people on the streets at all times of the day and night. How in the hell do you hide a body and no one sees it until the next morning?"

Dobbs straightened in his chair with a new light in his eyes. "You don't. You're right, Jackson. Someone had to have seen what happened. They either think what they saw is nothing, that it's their drunken imagination, or, they're running scared and won't talk to the cops. Plus, there's camera surveillance everywhere."

He glanced at Tara. "We need the media's help. We need them to ask the New Yorkers for any information they might have about this case. We might get leads we'd otherwise miss out on."

Tara grimaced. "Yeah, that should bring the crazies out of the woodworks. But I agree. It won't hurt to try. It's worked for us before. Let's talk to the Chief to see if a small reward can be offered. "

* * *

By noon all of New York's television and radio stations had broadcast the breaking news that Tara and Dobbs had released to them earlier. Chief Haynes had been able to come up with a $5,000 dollar reward from a well-known crime investigation team who had a weekly TV show to bring criminals to justice. Another team was set up at headquarters to take all calls on leads concerning the murder cases.

Tara and Dobbs didn't stick around to watch the news.

Another murder had been committed.

CHAPTER TWENTY-TWO

By six o'clock Monday evening, the local news anchors and newspaper reporters had a new name to add to their list of victims. News alerts were blasting from the networks, asking for the New Yorkers' help in finding the killer. The latest had already been identified by her grieving father.

Twenty-four-year old, Jessica Alise Nelson, a young, beautiful, dark-haired high school cheerleading instructor had been found in an alley behind a dumpster, killed the same way as their other victims and only two blocks over from Angie, his last victim.

He'd struck again. And fast.

While Jackson and his team were knocking on doors and questioning people on the streets close to the murder scene, Tara and Dobbs stood in front of their crime board once again. Tara pinned the picture of Jessica onto the board and stepped back to study what they had so far. Her gazed darted from each girl, victims from the present and past. They all looked enough alike that they could be family.

"What are we missing, Dobbs? I feel like we're letting them down. I keep thinking the murderer is trying to tell us something, and we're overlooking it."

Dobbs put an arm around her, pulling her to his side. She looked up and saw his jaw clench as he stared at the board. "We won't let them down. We're not stopping until we catch the bastard."

She shook off her fears. "Hell no, we're not." But, would it be in time to stop him killing again? She hoped so. "Until, we hear back from Jackson and forensics, there's not much else we can do tonight. Let's call it a night. I don't know about you, but I need a quick shower and different clothes before we meet everyone at the Pig Sty in less than two hours."

"Yep, I need to get prettied up and smelling good before I see Sandy." Dobbs grinned and flipped her hair before heading toward the door.

"Ah, you're already pretty, Dobbs. You want to borrow a pair of my high heels and a dress? Maybe some mascara to make your long eye lashes pop?"

Dobbs turned and took a step toward her, shaking a finger back and forth in her face. "Uh uh…once again, you have questioned my manhood. I'm thinking you're daring me to prove to you how much of a man I am, because you want me. You want me bad." He took another step forward with a mischievous twinkle in his eyes.

Her hand went up in a 'Stop' mode. "You take another step forward and my knee is going to take away the little bit of manhood you do have, my friend."

Then she darted around him and ran like hell.

His laughter mingled with hers as she slowed her steps down to normal in the hallway and past the officers in the bullpen. They were use to her and Dobb's constant banter to release the stress, but there was no need in interrupting the tired officer's card game.

And, she needed to get home. Jake was waiting.

* * *

A few minutes before eight, Tara and Jake entered Sandy's bar. For a Monday night, the bar was doing a fairly good business. They saw their group sitting around a long table near the back of the room and headed toward them.

Dobbs, Boyd Brennan, Jackson and Chief Haynes stood as they approached and greeted each other. Tara sat, and the others resumed their seats just as Sandy wearing her PIG STY t-shirt approached with a tray of bottled beer. Dispensing the drinks, she sat close beside Dobbs.

Chief Haynes took a long swallow and pointed the bottle neck toward Tara. "We were just talking about your Dad. Or, I should say Brennan and I were reminiscing about our detective days. Those were definitely the good ol' days. I was telling Brennan you've got your Dad's seriousness and wittiness along with your mom's beauty.

"That Rose was one sweet and lovely woman. Rob was one hell of a lucky guy back when I knew him." Brennan added.

The chief nodded. "True. And, Tara here is just as determined and skilled as Rob when it comes to hunting the killers."

"Thank you. That means a lot to me." Tara's cheeks burned over the compliments. She was used to a combative and dangerous occupation, of being one of the boys who didn't receive a lot of praise, except from Jake, and in his own way, Dobbs.

"I'm sure Dad was a lot more experienced." She took a long swig of her beer and looked down to keep them from seeing the tears she knew were in her eyes. *Dammit, I'm not going to let my emotions over their deaths ruin this night. I'm tired of feeling the never-ending grief I've felt all these years. For tonight at least, I want to know and remember the good parts of my parents.* Tara reigned in her dark thoughts and glanced back at the group with a saucy smile. "Just maybe not as pig-headed."

Jake laughed. "You said it, babe."

Dobbs snorted. "That's the damn truth." Sandy's elbow connected with his ribs, and his laughter turned into a groan. He glanced from his date and then the others seated around the table. "Hey. You don't have to work with her. I do. And, that wasn't a criticism. Her determination has helped us get several murderers off the street. I couldn't ask for a better partner."

"Sandy, what have you done to Dobbs?" Tara asked. "Have you drugged him or something? He's acting weird." She turned and gave Jake a stern look. "And, I'll deal with you later, bub." Her bogus expression of outrage ignited a spurt of laughter around the table including Jake's.

Sandy shrugged and smirked. "Not yet, but the night is young."

"May I recommend rat poison?"

"Bite me, Woods." Dobbs grinned.

Chief Haynes turned to Brennan. "See what I mean. Just like her Dad."

Brennan leaned back in his chair and nodded. "Yep. Just like Rob. Always joking, teasing, but serious as hell when he needed to be. Do you remember when we had a suspect in custody who we believed killed his wife? The Waskin case? We thought he was guilty without a doubt, but Rob wasn't convinced the husband did it."

Chief Haynes nodded. "How could I forget? He worked non-stop for days going over and over all the files we had on Waskin until he found the one thing that would prove his innocence. He found the true murderer. We thought he was wasting his time, but he proved us wrong."

"How?" Tara was absorbed in their story, her dad's story.

Brennan finished his beer and Sandy signaled to the bartender for another round for the table.

Brennan continued. "The wife had a secret lover that Waskin knew nothing about. When Waskin's wife wouldn't leave her husband, the lover killed her out of a jealous rage and planned on killing Waskin as well. We actually saved his life by arresting him and holding him for forty-eight hours. Woods dug deeper and found a couple of witnesses who led him to the lover and then his arrest. If it hadn't been for your dad's pig-headiness as you put it, we would have convicted an innocent man to possibly a death sentence."

Tara's heart contracted. They were talking about her dad, her idol. Her heart-warm thoughts were interrupted as an older, pudgy man approached their table bringing them another tray full of beer. As he passed the drinks around, she noticed that his hollow eyes looked like he'd seen hell and was crawling out of a burning purgatory, His gaze focused on her and he almost dumped the drinks in her lap. She scooted back just in time. She'd never seen him in the bar before, but he looked familiar somehow. When he left, she shook off an uneasiness. Leaning over to Sandy, she whispered, "Who's that?"

Sandy whispered back. "That's Joe. He fell on hard times and needed a job, and I needed help. So, I gave him a chance today. So far, he's better than nothing."

"Barely."

Jake touched her arm and pointed at his watch. "We just have time to drink this one beer before our dinner reservation. Steak and Seafood is only a few blocks away."

"Sounds great." Brennan said. He raised his beer bottle in a toast. "Here's to the next generation of law enforcement of our dear friend who we will forever miss, Detective Rob Woods. May his wisdom, his bull-dog determination and his unconditional love follow in his footsteps with his child Tara and his future grandchildren. May God bless them all."

Beer bottles clicked. "Hear, Hear."

Tara prayed her over-emotional tears were hidden.

CHAPTER TWENTY-THREE

Tuesday morning, Tara rushed through her office door at eight-twenty. Dobbs was waiting.

"You're late."

"Sorry. I overslept." She walked around her desk and collapsed into her chair, actually glancing down to make sure she was completely dressed and wearing matching shoes. It was that kind of morning.

Her body and brain felt like she'd been in a fight and lost big time after tossing and turning all night. Her mind had mulled over every conversation from the dinner with her dad's friends. She'd absorbed every morsel of knowledge she'd learned about her parents from Brennan and Chief Haynes and couldn't wait until they met again so she could grill them further.

Her busy thoughts dissipated as her partner's abrupt movement drew her back into the moment. Swinging his feet off the desk, Dobbs walked over to the coffee bar and cleared his throat to get her attention. Then he swept a 'ta-da!' hand motion over the bar.

Tara's gaze followed and her eyes widened. An excited grin spread across her face. "Oh my God. Are you frickin' serious?" A state of the art, two pot coffeemaker with a full brewed pot of coffee sat in the spot beside the cups, stirrers and creamer. "What the heck, Dobbs? Who bought this beauty? I know it's not in our precinct budget."

Dobbs gave her a big smile without answering. He poured her a cup of coffee and freshened his own. He carried both back to the desk and handed Tara hers before sitting back down. He shrugged nonchalantly and stretched his long legs out in front of him. He glanced her way and tried to rearrange his grin into a mock scowl. "You look like a little girl on Christmas morning. It's nothing to get excited about. I just thought we both could use a good cup of coffee this morning, so, I stopped on my way to work and picked up a coffee maker in case we have to pull an all-nighter again. No big deal."

He was trying too hard to appear laid-back and unfazed by her excitement over a fresh cup of strong coffee, instead of the bitter, watered down version from the machine. She knew he'd done it for her, to help her through the emotional roller coaster she'd ridden after discussing her parents the night before. Instead of a friendly, supportive hug, he'd bought her a coffee pot. Typical of Dobbs. She couldn't ask for a better partner and friend. Not, that she would ever tell him. His head was big enough.

She decided to let him off the hook and refrained from teasing him as she'd normally do. Instead, she raised her coffee cup in a salute. Bringing the cup of dark, pure heaven to her lips, she blew on the hot liquid, then took a sip. She sighed in ecstasy. "Damn, Dobbs. This is good. Thank you. You don't realize how much I need this."

The corners of his lips curled into a reluctant smile. "You're welcome. Are you awake enough to work on the case, or do you need the whole pot to revive you?"

Tara let him change the subject. They needed all their attention on the killer on the loose who had to be found. "I'm awake." She stood, retrieved the pot and refilled their cups. Going back to her desk, she asked, "Have you heard from Jackson or Melinda this morning?"

Dobbs shook his head. "No. Not yet. I thought we could talk to them together." He took his phone out of his shirt pocket, dialed Jackson's number and put him on speaker phone.

Jackson answered on the first ring. He sounded frustrated when Dobbs asked if he had anything for them. "I have nothing to report. Man, do you know how many cameras there are in the neighborhood where the last victim was found? So far, I've watched twenty hours of tapes from the store merchants and street camera surveillances from around the time of the last murder. I'm concentrating solely on the dumpster footage where she was found. Nothing yet. I'll spread out to other areas if I don't find anything."

"Smart," Tara agreed. "There's got to be something the cameras picked up."

"A person can't be in this area without being filmed. I'm not leaving until I find who we're looking for, even if I have to pack a suitcase and temporarily move into a store's back_room and watch every tape over and over until I find him. My other officers have interviewed the nearby store owners and any pedestrians walking anywhere close to the alley and dumpster. They're following all leads mentioned. Again, nothing."

"I think you're right, Jackson," Tara said. "The cameras should be your main focus. Pull in as many officers as you need to go over those tapes. Put as many eyes on them as you can. And check the tapes from say....ten hours earlier than you looked at before."

"That would be during daylight. Would he be that brave?" Jackson asked.

"Brave? No. Crazy? Yes," Tara replied. "I'll check with Cindy and ask her to come up with a new profile layout of our perp, but as we mentioned before, it's possible his actions are escalating. He may be getting to the point where he thinks he's invincible and can't be caught and punished. Maybe his recklessness is more exciting. Who knows? It does seem like he's needing his pleasure oftener. The murders are happening faster than usual."

Dobbs added. "But, he isn't getting any more violent. His actions with the victims haven't changed.

Same M.O. thirty years ago as today. So far, he's eluded us. We can only hope he gets cocky and starts leaving evidence behind."

Tara blew out a deep breath and nodded. "We need some good luck for a change." They had nothing but dead ends to work on and they were getting nowhere with any new leads they'd uncovered. "Okay. Jackson, we don't have any other choice. We need you to stay put and continue watching the footage. He's not a freakin' ghost. He had to physically carry his last victim from his vehicle and put her in that spot. It took time to arrange her body into his favorite position. It's important to him. I think he would've clipped on the bows and barrettes before he moved her, since they wouldn't be disturbed during the move, but, he wouldn't take the chance of the doll falling out while he moved her. He'd place it inside her after he laid her beside the dumpster and had her arranged. That's time, guys. Time that someone could've spotted him, but, he wasn't worried. Why?"

Dobbs straightened in his chair. "Holy hell. He wasn't worried about being seen, because he had a reason to be there."

Tara's pulse raced. "A uniform? You think he works for the City Sanitation department?"

"Or, works in the store that has use of the dumpster, and he takes out the trash every day," Dobbs continued.

"Jackson. Talk to us. Have you seen anyone like this on tape?" Tara sat on the edge of her chair.

"Maybe," Jackson answered cautiously. "I need to watch them again with the store owner to be sure.

There were a couple of employees on different shifts who I'd questioned but marked off my list because the owner vouched for them. The time on the footage only showed around a five minute time span between when one of the guys left to dump the trash and went back inside. That wouldn't have given him enough time to arrange the body. The other employee on the footage was behind the counter waiting on a customer while the trash was being taken out."

"What we're looking for is someone who belonged, who would've come from behind the store carrying something heavy. He could've hidden the body in a blanket or bag until he got there. Remember, the victims bleed out before he moves them, so there are no bloody bags for someone to see and report. Where do the store employees park?" Dobbs leaned in closer to his phone.

Jackson took a moment to answer as the question sunk in. Disbelief strained his voice. "In the parking lot behind the store. The only place on the whole damn street where there are no cameras."

"Well, hell."

CHAPTER TWENTY-FOUR

Tara paced the floor, her thoughts on the phone conversation with Jackson. Were they finally on to something? Had the killer parked in back of the store where he maybe worked, dumped the body, placed it in a specific position and driven away without anyone seeing him?

Even so, he would've left tire tracks and footprints behind. The lab would need to be called in again to gather sample tire and shoe powder castings from the parking lot pavement. It was a shot in the dark that they would find the one set of tires or shoe tracks left behind by the killer, and it would mean several man hours by the lab techs to find the exact match mixed in with all of the other tracks, but it was worth a shot.

"He would've left the body, retraced his steps back to his car, gotten in and driven off. If we can match the shoe impressions to that particular tire tread, we'd at least know which tracks to investigate. The treads might identify the type of vehicle he was driving." Fingers crossed, Tara thought.

Dobbs stopped his own pacing and glanced her way. "We're on the same brain wave. I was thinking along the same lines. A K-9 will need to be brought in to sniff either the murderer or Jessica Nelson's scent. I'll give the lab a call and get them out there."

"They'll need to do a dirt analysis on the treads, too," Tara said. "We need to know where else he'd been last night. If we could be so lucky, the type of dirt on the tires might lead us to the area where he lives or where the latest victim was murdered. Or at least, a close proximity."

Dobbs reached for his cell phone and punched in numbers.

While he gave his directives to the forensic lab, Tara called the chief to update him. Even though he'd given them complete access to all departments in their precinct for this case, she respected him enough to keep him informed. As usual, he gave his full support and approved any overtime they needed. His only response was, "Do whatever you need to take the s.o.b off the streets."

"Yes sir." Tara grinned and hung up. The chief only cursed when he was deeply frustrated over a case. And, this case had bitten him in the butt for thirty years.

Ending his call, Dobbs refilled their coffee cups before returning back to his seat and focusing his gaze on the crime board. "The lab said to give them a few days to get back with us on the prints. They're putting a rush on it."

Tara groaned. She knew it took time for the lab work to be completed, but that didn't mean she liked it. "The killer is not going to give us a few days before he murders, again." She wished for the day when new technology allowed it to be done quicker.

"We don't have a choice. Our only hope is that Jackson can find something on the security tapes we can run with. Like a clear mug shot on the footage or something." He gripped his Styrofoam coffee cup hard enough to crush it. Luckily, it was empty. He threw the damaged cup into the trashcan and blew out a sharp breath.

Dobbs didn't lose his cool often, but, this case was getting to him as much as it was to her. At least his relationship with Sandy hadn't softened him up which could be a major problem in their line of work. It could turn into a life or death situation for both of them at a time they needed level heads. But, Dobbs was one partner she didn't have to worry about getting soft. He may get down, but not out, nor soft.

She could say the same for herself and Jake's relationship. Dobbs needs her to be completely focused and tough while on a murder case. No time for sentimental bull from either. "Careful there, Rambo. Don't waste that steel grip on a flimsy coffee cup when there's a bastard running free who deserves it more." She smiled at him over the rim of her cup.

Dobbs shook his head and shot her a small, devilish grin. She watched in amusement as he plopped his boots on top of her desk and scooted his butt back into his seat to get comfortable. "I can't wait."

"Nor, I. We're depending on Jackson, now."

"Yep. But until we hear from him, there are a few things we can still do. Let's see what Melinda has for us."

While they waited on Jackson and forensics to do what they did best, Dobbs dialed Melinda's office phone and put the call on speaker.

She answered on the second ring. "Hey guys. I was getting ready to call you. I've got some information for you. It could be good or bad. I guess it depends on how you look at it."

Dobbs chuckled. "You know us. We're always the optimistic. Give it to us. Tell us something we want to hear."

"I'll try. While I was trying to link similar homicides between your cases here in New York and any in New Jersey, I ran the multiple victims' statistics on all homicide databases. I upped it to include all fifty states. No other police departments or governments have listed any murders similar to ours. Ever. Including New Jersey. Our guy is staying in New York, my friends."

Silence. Then, Dobbs spoke. "Well, it was worth checking out. Thanks Melinda. Do you happen to know if the NJPD has the Mustang's forensics ready?"

"It's been processed, but there was no luck in identifying the DNA or prints other than the owner,

Walt Landers who willingly provided his prints. Another set of blurred prints belongs to the mechanic who'd changed the oil months ago. Nothing in the databases matches any of the others prints we've collected."

"Not finding a match doesn't mean crap if our killer hasn't been arrested before and isn't in the database, yet." Dobbs ran his hands through his hair.

"Sorry. Wish I had more for you." Melinda told them.

Dobb's sighed. "No, I'm sorry. Just getting frustrated. This creep just keeps jerking our chain. You've done a superb job. Appreciate it."

"Thanks Dobbs. I'll keep looking."

"Let us know if you find anything."

"Will do."

The phone call ended, and they were no closer to their suspect.

CHAPTER TWENTY-FIVE

Later that Tuesday morning, Dobbs glanced at his watch and rubbed his tired eyes. He put down the files he was studying and glanced at Tara. "It's almost ten o'clock. Reading these profile sheets for the fiftieth time isn't getting us anywhere. Why don't we give Jackson a hand looking over the footage? I hate waiting."

Tara closed the folder in front of her and rose to her feet. "I'm with you. There's nothing else we can do here. We might see something he's unaware of since he's been out in the field. We haven't updated him in a while."

"Let me give Sandy a quick call before we leave. She should be up by now. I told her I'd call her to remind her to pick up her clothes from the cleaners before she went into work this evening."

Tara's eyes lit up and she sat back down. "Ah. Getting domestic, I see. Tell her 'hi' for me."

Dobbs raised an eyebrow, but ignored her dig. A slight curve of his lip told her she could expect a payback later. She grinned and checked her phone messages while he made his call. She planned to eavesdrop.

He dialed Sandy's number. After the sixth ring, he left a message and hung up. "She didn't answer. Probably in the shower. I'll give her a call later. You ready?"

"Yes. And, you're buying lunch."

He motioned for her toward the door. "I bought the last time. It's your turn."

"In that case, we're eating drive-thru burgers without fries. I'm saving my money for a new stove with a double oven and a larger fridge."

"Why? I mean, it's just you and Jake. You eat a lot, but not that much."

Her steps slowed and her cheeks heated. Uncomfortable, she shrugged and turned around to face him. "You won't make fun of me if I tell you?"

He stared deep into her eyes. His expression softened and he turned serious. "Of course not. Not when it seems to be this important to you."

Her feet shuffled. Her gaze dropped. What was happening to her? She'd teased Dobbs about becoming domestic when she was just as bad or worse. A few months ago, she would've never had these strong familial feelings that didn't include her parents.

Her Mom and Dad wouldn't be forgotten by her. Ever. But she had another type of family now. Some who had known her parents, and some who hadn't and none of them were blood related. And she had Jake. And Dobbs.

Last night, Detective Brennan and Chief Haynes had helped her frozen heart thaw some with their serious and sometimes funny stories about her mom and dad. They'd known them longer and better than she did, which was painful, but also encouraging. Her parents seemed more real, more human through the eyes of the grownup she'd become.

Forcing her thoughts back to their conversation, she said, "I was thinking how nice it would be to have a good home-cooked meal for everyone close to me and Jake during the Thanksgiving and Christmas holidays. It would be more meaningful than eating out in a restaurant." She shrugged and sighed. "No big deal. Am I getting too sentimental and gushy for a New York Detective?"

Dobbs smiled and placed an arm around her shoulder. "Not at all. As long as you invite Sandy and me. Turkey and cornbread dressing?"

Her heart swelled in relief. He was making light of her concerns. "Most definitely, plus stuffing inside the turkey for the ones who prefer it over the dressing, and all the side dishes. Jake and I will do it together. I'll invite your family and Jake's, and our other friends. Our apartment is small, but I think we can fit everyone in without a problem. Maybe? I might need a bigger table." Her voice rose along with her excitement.

Dobbs laughed. "As long as you don't make me sit outside by the snow-covered pool to eat or make me sick with food poisoning, I'm fine. I'm not worried, though. Jake will keep the food safe and you have a few months to prepare. I know Jake will help and I'm volunteering Sandy and me to help. It sounds wonderful. Count us in."

Tara nodded while she lassoed in her emotions. Swallowing back the lump in her throat, she bumped her shoulder against his arm. "That means a lot."

Before he could reply, her phone rang. She glanced at the displayed number. "It's Jackson." She cleared her throat, her voice already emotional and spoke into the phone. Seconds later, she disconnected and turned to Dobbs. Her words rushed out and her excitement mounted. "Let's go. Jackson thinks he's found our man."

* * *

Thirty minutes later, Tara and Dobbs sat in the back of the convenience store office surrounded with boxes and boxes of inventory. The manager, Dean Carlson, a man in his fifties wearing thick, round glasses, sat behind his cluttered desk wringing his hands. The dark-brown paneling on the walls caused the man's pale complexion to look even bleaker. He rubbed his forehead. "How in the hell am I going to explain to our customers that a dead woman was dumped behind the store? They'll be too scared to shop here anymore. Plus, my boss in Chicago is demanding immediate damage control or I'll lose my job."

Tara wanted nothing more than to see what Jackson had found, but she needed the manager calm and cooperative. "Tell your boss you have the NYPD here to help with the damage control. We'll catch the guy who did this and then the public won't have a reason to be afraid, okay? Your boss might even give you a raise."

Carlson straightened in his chair and adjusted his glasses. Her words seemed to hit home and he calmed somewhat. "From your lips to his ears. Thanks, Detective. How can I help you?"

"You're helping by letting us watch the tapes from here. We appreciate it. Now, Jackson, go ahead."

Jackson pushed in the tape he wanted them to watch and set the camera footage to run from the beginning. While fast forwarding through the unimportant parts, he filled them in on what he'd found.

"We lucked out big time. The store across the street has a camera positioned to film their store front which captures the alley with our dumped victim. The owner let me bring the tape over here after I called you."

"That's good of him. Tell him we appreciate his help. I assume his tape is the one we're watching?" Dobbs watched as the tape rolled, showing a nice, clean shopping area in the older section of the borough. The videotape showed heavy foot traffic on both sides of the street, lasting well into the late evening. The twenty-four hour, brick-front convenience store they were in had a steady flow of customers shopping and buying everything from toilet paper to beer.

"Yes. I won't bore you with the film showing the trash being taken out but I'll tell you about it, instead. Carlson here told me his employee who took out the trash around ten Sunday night stated there was no body by the dumpster and the other employee confirmed, which means that the latest victim, the Nelson girl, could've only been dumped sometime between ten Sunday night and eight Monday morning when the garbage collectors arrived to dump the bin and discovered the body. So, I've been viewing all footage in that time frame. And, here it is." Jackson slowed the film and pointed at the monitor.

Tara leaned in closer for a better view. The time on the film showed three-seventeen Monday morning. Out of the dark alley, a person appeared on the tape. Definitely a short, overweight male, bent over at the waist and carrying something heavy. His back was to the camera. He knelt on one knee and carefully placed the heavy looking object on the ground in front of the dumpster. He spent a couple of minutes doing something. Then, nodding to himself as if he was satisfied with his work, he stood.

"Hold on," Jackson said. "He turns toward the camera in a minute. Wait for it. And, there he is!"

Tara jumped up from her chair. "That's the same guy who attacked me in the parking lot. The moonlight makes him just as clear here as he did that night. And, I can tell he's the same guy we saw last night working at the Pig Sty. Sandy had just hired him. She said he was down on his luck. Dobbs, what was his name?"

Dobbs' fingers dug into the chair's armrest. "Joe is the only name I heard. Hell, I don't think she gave a last name."

Carlson spoke up. "He's not a 'Joe'. His name is Ben Staffer, or that's the name he gave me when he applied. He works the second shift, eleven to seven for me."

"Did he work last night?" Dobbs stood and paced, keeping his gaze on Carlson.

"He did. The other employee working that shift said he clocked out the second his time was up. Said he had to get somewhere fast. He never mentioned another job to me, though."

Tara's thoughts raced. "The Pig Sty is only about twenty minutes away from here. The time frame would allow him to work here, choose his next victim and still make it to the bar on time."

"And, off work from the bar in time to hunt and kill afterwards," Dobbs added with growing excitement showing in his eyes.

"Right. Jackson, we need his employment file with addresses, phone numbers, license plate numbers, etc., then run his profile by Melinda to see if he has any priors."

"Will do."

Tara raised a hand. "Jackson, wait. Dammit. I knew that name sounded familiar. Isn't that Walt Landers' stepbrother? The one mentioned in the cold case report. Remember, Dobbs?"

"My God, you're right. Jackson, it would be quicker to check with Landers to see if he's heard from his stepbrother lately or knows where he might be living."

"I'm on it."

When Jackson followed the manager out of his office, Tara shot a glance at her partner. "Get Sandy on the phone."

"Already on it." His trembling fingers auto-dialed.

CHAPTER TWENTY-SIX

Locking the Pig Sty's door behind her at closing time Monday night, Sandy was feeling excited to meet up with Dobbs, later. She whistled a happy tune and heard the lock click in place. Then, she smelled a sickly, sweet odor. Before she could react, a soaked rag smothered her mouth and nose. She struggled. Then, she knew nothing.

* * *

Sandy woke up with a sudden jerk, disoriented and scared. How long had she been out, and where was she? Like a slow running film, she replayed the last few minutes as she left the bar.

And, the overpowering smell. That's when her memory eluded her.

Scared to, but scared not to, she eased her eyes open and looked around. The unfamiliar, brightly lit room was pink. Pink walls. Pink carpet. Pink headboard with a pink comforter and shams. Dolls of all sizes clothed in pink frilly dresses sat on shelves in a cabinet standing ceiling high. A pink brush capturing dark strands of hair along with several pink bows and headbands sat on top of a dusty, pink dresser. A dark-pink blind with curtains covered the one small window in the room, leaving her with no way to know if it was night or day.

Holy hell, who lived here? The makers of Pepto Bismol?

She tried to scramble up but fell back hard against the pillow. Glancing up, she realized why. Her hands were bound above her head. Her heartbeat tripled in time. Short, erratic breaths rushed through her nostrils. The other end of the tight rope was attached above her head to the pink leather headboard.

She struggled in earnest with the small, braided rope tied around her wrists. The only result was burns on her wrists. Swinging her legs to the side, she managed to get them over the side of the bed, but they were still inches away from the floor. She scooted her butt closer to the edge, but the rope kept her from moving more than a couple more inches. Not enough for her feet to touch the floor and stand.

Nauseated from the chloroform still in her system, her stomach rolled. She cried out, her panic rising. "Help me. Is anyone here? Hello?" No answer. Frightened out of her mind, her adrenalin kicked in. "Look, I'm going to throw up all over your pretty pink shit if you don't get in here and untie me. And, it will not be pretty."

The bedroom door slammed back on its hinges. Sandy's heart skipped a fierce beat. The same short, chunky man she'd recently hired at her bar stood in the doorway with both hands covering his ears.

He stormed into the room shouting, his face blood red. "Shut the hell up, Mother. Shut up. I can't stand to hear your shrieking voice. Please, shut up." Joe, her new employee paced back and forth at the foot of the bed.

A chill like she'd never experienced before ran down her spine. He was nuts. When she'd awakened a few minutes earlier, from the chloroform haze, she'd experienced absolute, bone-jerking fear. She hadn't known where she was, how long she'd been there or what type of lunatic she'd be facing when he decided to show up. Now, she knew. Demented. The worst possible kind. Now, she knew true fear.

Fear wouldn't keep her alive, though. She had to keep her wits. If she could get him to untie her hands, she might have a slight chance. Adrenaline kicked in. She kept her voice calm and soothing. "Look Joe, you've made a horrible mistake. I'm not your mother. I'm Sandy, the one who gave you a job when you were down on your luck. I helped you. Remember? Detective Dobbs and Detective Woods are good friends of mine. You met them last night. Everyone from the Police Department to the FBI will be looking for me. It would be best for you to let me go before they get here."

He grinned evilly, his eyes vacant, and shook his head. "My name's not really Joe. I lied. You can call me Ben now. I'll make sure you will never be able to tell anyone my true identity."

Sandy's brain digested his fanatical words. Her heartbeat stopped for a split second. "You're going to regret it."

Nothing.

"Look, at least untie me. I'm not going anywhere. I really need to use the bathroom." And, a distraction.

A gleeful cackle erupted, and he stopped pacing near her head. Too damn close. As he studied her, his features turned sinister. His hand flew out and his palm slammed against her cheek. He screamed out, "Another one of your lies, Mother."

Sandy's head bounced against the pillow. Her cheek burned as if he'd put a hot coal against it. She bit her lip to keep from crying out. Her gut told her he was waiting for any sign of weakness from her.

He'd be waiting a hell of a long time.

The creep jerked her head up by her hair. She yelped and struggled.

"Stop fighting me." He jerked harder and slipped a long leash around her neck before untying her hands.

"Get up. I'm going to let you go to the bathroom, but the door stays open. If you try anything, I'll snap your damn neck. Do you understand?"

Breathing hard, she gave him a 'go to hell' look but nodding. With wobbly knees, she slid off the bed. He led her to a small bathroom with rusty pipes and filth that made her stand up to do her business while he stood out of sight. Her stomach rolled again. She turned and emptied her stomach in the commode. When the nausea finally abated, she straightened and stumbled to the sink. She splashed water on her face, taking care not to touch the bruises on her face. She washed her hands and opted to use her t-shirt to dry her face and hands instead of the filthy towel hanging on the towel rack. She looked around for any way to escape. Nothing. There was no window, and she didn't see anything she could use as a weapon. Her shoulders slumped.

He jerked on the leash. "Hurry up."

As she passed him, she snarled, "I'm going to kill you, you bastard."

He only laughed and jerked again, forcing her to walk out on her own before he dragged her out. "Get back on the bed."

When she climbed back onto the bed, he tied her hands back to the headboard. Leaving the leash hanging around her neck, he walked out.

Sandy pulled on the ropes around her wrists again, jerking and twisting until they began to bleed. Frustrated tears fell as she struggled with no success. She couldn't give up and let the bastard win. The alternative wasn't an option. She didn't want to die. "Dobbs, I need you."

"You're wasting your time. No one will ever find you here." Ben stood in the doorway holding a tray. "I made you a bowl of oatmeal. I'm going to untie one of your hands to let you eat, but if you try anything stupid, I'll snap your neck in two."

Sandy scooted up in the bed and watched him warily while he placed the tray on the bedside table. He picked up the leash and pulled it tight before untying her right hand. Then he placed the tray in her lap.

"Where am I? What time is it?"

"Don't worry about where you are. It's nine o'clock. Not that it matters."

"Morning or night?

"Morning. Now, eat. It's your favorite." He stood at the end of the bed and watched her, waited.

Her stomach rolled. She swallowed down the rising bile in her throat. Hoping her stomach was empty from her sickness earlier, she put the spoon of the maple oatmeal to her lips. The sickly, sweet smell almost did her in, but she took a small bite and forced it down. Wondering if his kitchen was as dirty as his bathroom, she almost gagged again, but knew she had to keep up her strength to fight. She took another bite and then another until she was finished. Drinking the glass of warm, murky water sitting beside the bowl, she pushed the tray away.

"Good, Mommy. I knew you'd love your breakfast. It's your favorite." He retied her hands and took the tray away.

Moments later, her eyes drooped, her mind became fuzzy and her body grew limp. Oh God. He'd drugged her. She fought it, but the drug was too strong.

* * *

Shortly before noon, Tara and Dobbs stood outside Sandy's abandoned car in the 'Pig Sty's' parking lot. Dobbs had made the twenty-minute drive from the convenience store to the bar in fifteen minutes, sirens blasting. Tara held on with one hand while calling for backup.

Blue lights bounced off the building and the few vehicles in the bar's parking lot, giving off an eerie illusion even in the bright daylight.

Sandy's manager, Joey, stood beside them. He'd made the frantic call to Dobbs earlier, informing him that something was wrong. He said he'd arrived at the bar at his usual time and found the backdoor unlocked with Sandy's keys still inserted. Her purse was lying on the ground. Her car was sitting in the parking lot, and she was nowhere to be found.

While Tara called the chief to inform him Sandy was missing, other police officers and investigators were already arriving to work the scene. Bystanders and Pig Sty employees lingered outside the bar whispering and wondering, Had the pervert struck again? Fear vibrated throughout the growing crowd.

Dobbs clenched his cell phone in his hand, his words rushing out as soon as Jackson answered. "Jackson, I want every available body on this. Staffer may have Sandy. He has to be found."

A long pause filled the air waves. "I'm on it. I'll get back with you as soon as I have something. I haven't been able to locate Landers, and he's not answering his phone. The manager tried to pull Staffer's employee file and it's missing. Melinda is looking on her database for his address as we speak."

"Thanks, Jackson. I need your expertise now more than ever."

"You've got it." The call went dead.

Frustrated and feeling helpless, Dobbs and Tara studied the scene. Sandy's car sat in the parking lot. The doors were locked as usual and looked untouched. Her cell phone rang inside her purse when he'd called the number a few minutes earlier. Her credit cards and cash were inside her wallet. Nothing seemed to be missing other than Sandy.

There was no sign of a struggle. No blood. Sandy's or the perv's. But Dobbs would bet his sweet ass she'd struggled. She wouldn't have gone willingly, unless, she was unconscious, hurt or dead.

Dobbs ran his hand across the top of his head and cursed. Why in the hell hadn't he checked on her earlier, when she hadn't answer her phone? Way too much time had passed.

Worry overrode his anger. His wide, strong shoulders drooped. "She never made it home last night," he said, glancing over at Tara. "I should've insisted on her coming home with me even when she told me she had things to do at her apartment this morning. I should've at least waited at the bar to take her home and spent the night with her. Dammit, she'd be safe if I had."

Tara touched his arm. "It's not your fault. The bastard had her staked out. He planned on Sandy being his next victim. If it hadn't been last night, it would've been another time and place."

Dobbs jaw clenched. "Well, I have plans, too. I'll find Sandy and that bastard if it's the last thing I ever do. I swear, he'll never hurt another woman, again."

Tara nodded and reached for her phone. "I'm with you, but we can't do anything more here. Let's see if Melinda has found an address on this Staffer guy."

Five minutes later, they finally got a bit of good luck. Melinda had found Staffer's address and conviction record. She texted the information to Tara's phone.

Tara read the text out loud to Dobb and smiled. "You may have your chance to find them sooner than you thought. Let's go."

Running to the car, Dobbs started the motor, and he and Tara raced to Staffer's address.

CHAPTER TWENTY-SEVEN

Sandy moaned and opened her gritty eyes. She closed them tight as a bright light pierced her vision. The blinds were raised, and the sun was shining into the room. She opened her eyes cautiously, hoping to see out the window. Her heart sank. From what she could see, there was nothing but a grove of trees outside.

No highway. No traffic. No one. She was no longer in the bustling downtown of Manhattan. Where was she?

Thoughts of the morning before and the man who kidnapped her crashed into her mind and fear returned in full force. It didn't matter where she was. No one would find her in time. Unless, she found a way to rescue herself.

But, she'd paid close attention to Dobbs and Tara when they talked about their newest case. This Ben had to be their serial killer. Too many similarities such as the dolls and pink shit. It was him. And, she knew the fate of the other victims.

But, not her. Damn it. Not her. She had to think. What would Dobbs and Tara do?

Choking back tears, she realized she'd been knocked out for hours. Her head pounded and her mouth felt as dry as the desert. Her stomach churned. She groaned and tried to sit up. The drugs had weakened her.

Hearing a faint noise, Sandy jerked her head to the other side of the room and gasped in shock. There he sat beside her bed. Her heart pounded out of control. Her eyes widened, and she sank back into the pillows in fear and revulsion.

Ben wore a long, dark wig with a pink barrette on the side. He was dressed in a long, old-fashioned, pink evening gown and shiny black leather Mary Jane shoes. He had smeared pink lipstick across his lips. His legs were crossed at the ankles and his hands clasped together in his lap. He smiled. "You're finally awake. It's time to play dress up, Mommy."

Holy shit.

* * *

Tara and Dobbs reached Staffer's apartment fifteen minutes later. Five minutes after that, the manager was convinced to open his tenant's door without a warrant.

"He's a weird dude, anyway," the manager explained while unlocking the door. "I'll be thrilled to get rid of him. Hopefully, he'll be thrown in jail for a long time for whatever he's done, and I can rent the room to someone else."

Biting at the bit to get inside, Tara pushed the door open. "You might get your wish."

She and Dobbs entered the apartment, guns drawn. They swept the four rooms in the apartment that consisted of a small, outdated kitchen, living room, bedroom and bathroom. They found no one.

Mail, and a newspaper dated from the day before, lay on the kitchen counter. One coffee cup and a crusted cereal bowl sat in the sink. Otherwise, the apartment was neat. The very minimum of cheap furniture filled the rooms, that looked bare without any pictures on the wall or photos sitting around. Two shirts with the convenience store's logo on the pocket and one pair of jeans hung in the closet.

Tara replaced her gun into its holster. She glanced around the kitchen with her hands on her hips. "This isn't his permanent home. He's using this place as a fake address to give to his employers or whoever."

As usual, Dobb's thoughts were closely following hers. "Because, he lives somewhere else and that's probably where he's taking his victims."

Tara's heart sank. "But, where?"

* * *

Late Tuesday morning, Tara sat at her desk facing Dobbs, and rubbing her gritty eyes. More than twenty-four hours of face stubble, wrinkled clothes and eyes red from hours without sleep showed his own exhaustion. But what they felt was nothing compared to what Sandy must be going through, he thought. If she was still alive. His fingers clenched and he forced the inconceivable thought out of his mind. She had to be okay.

Tara shifted in her chair. She ran her fingers through her hair and swore. "I hate waiting. Landers has been no help in giving us his step-brother's recent address. Sounds like he's skipped the country. He's not answering his phone or knocks on his door. The neighbors says they haven't seen him in a couple of days."

"He may just be away for a few days. We'll have Jackson continue to check on him."

"You're right. He'll want an update on his wrecked Mustang sooner or later. Until he does contact us, we know from Melinda that Staffer spent thirty years in prison for killing his mother. All we need now is for her to come through for us with all his known addresses before and after he was incarcerated for years."

Dobbs stood and began pacing the small office. "I feel so damned helpless."

Tara felt his pain. What if it was Jake in danger instead of Sandy? She would go ballistic. "I know, but, our best bet is to let Jackson's and Melinda's people do their jobs. It's what they do best. We need their Intel to know our next steps."

Without any warning, Detective Brennan stormed into her office and interrupted them. "Hey guys, Haynes updated me on your person of interest. After I left the chief's office, I got to thinking about something and rushed back. There's something about this Staffer guy that seems so familiar. I just can't put my finger on it, right now."

Dobbs stopped his pacing and went rushed back to Tara's desk. "I remember seeing his name in your files as next of kin to Landers. You guys brought him in and he was released." He picked up the cold case files and started flipping through the pages.

Brennan nodded. "Correct. I remember now. We interviewed him, but couldn't find anything that would stick in court. Landers' father married Staffer's mother. It was his father's third marriage. Staffer had a sister. I think her name was Patty. It should be in the files. She was killed in a car wreck when she was eight years, old. The mother was driving drunk."

Dobbs got out his phone and found the attachment he'd sent to Melinda with a picture of Staffer. He showed it to Brennan. "Do you recognize him as the one you investigated?"

Brennan studied the picture and nodded. "He's a lot older here, but it's him. That's not what's bugging the crap out of me, though. There's something else. His M.O. is right there in the back of my mind. I'll remember it in a little while. I'm older too and my memory isn't sharp as it used to be. When I was younger, we didn't have the databases we have now. Has Haynes seen his picture?"

Tara's excitement rose as she emailed the picture to the chief. Brennan's information was significant. "I just sent it to him. We were waiting to hear from Melinda before we updated the chief any further."

Brennan nodded and walked back out the door, calling over his shoulder, "I'm heading his way. Between the both of us we might remember."

* * *

Two hours later, Dobbs and Tara still had nothing. Dobbs threw his pen across the room and rubbed his face. "Sandy, my God, Sandy," he thought. "Please be safe. Do everything you can do, baby, until I can get to you."

His prayers stopped as Brennan and Haynes stormed into Tara's office. "I've got it." Brennan ran his hand through his red hair in excitement. A huge smile appeared on his freckled face. "Between me and Haynes, I knew we would remember, eventually."

Tara stood and leaned over her desk. "Don't keep us in suspense. Spill it."

Dobbs sat back in his chair. "What do you have?"

"I know his past."

"Talk to me," Dobbs said, leaning forward expectantly.

Brennan glanced at the notes in his hands. "It was the pink barrette that kept nagging at me, and then it hit me. Around thirty-five or so years, ago I remember my parents talking about a nutcase who killed his mother and buried her in his backyard. Haynes and I located the archived court documents and newspaper reports. That's what took us so long to get back to you. It says here that Ben Staffer was fourteen years old when he killed his mother. Living on the streets as a runaway, he got away with it for almost five years before he was captured and charged for her murder. His trial and sentencing happened less than two years after they found our last cold case victim. At the trial, he talked about how his mother had become mentally unstable after his eight-year-old sister was killed in a car accident. His mother was driving drunk when she wrecked the car. She blamed herself for her daughter's death. It was around that time that Phil Landers, the stepfather, left and filed for a divorce. That was the stick that broke the camel's back. Staffer's mother started dressing him up like his sister, with pink barrettes and dresses. She made him play with dolls. Then, she'd molest him. Over and over for years. He claims it started when he was around ten years old."

"Damn, I almost don't blame him for killing her. Sounds like the 'crazy' might run in the family," Tara said.

Brennan nodded. "None of us know what we'd be capable of if we were put in that position. Get this. His parole came up two months ago and he was released on good behavior."

Excitement burned through Dobb's veins. "That's around the time we found the first victim. I don't guess those papers tell you where he might have gone?"

"No, but, I can tell you where he and his mother lived. Her abandoned house is next to a wooded area about fifteen miles from where the victims were found. Here's the address."

Dobbs whooped out loud and leaped to his feet. He slapped Brennan on the back and grabbed his jacket. "Hell of a job, Brennan. And, you too, Chief Haynes.

We've nailed him. That's not far from here. Let's go."

* * *

Sandy shivered in revulsion as Staffers gently combed her hair, jerking her head from side to side. Angered, he grabbed a handful of her hair and pulled until she cried out. "Now quit or I'll put the rope back around your neck. I want to make you pretty, Mommy." He slid a pink, lacy headband onto her head.

"You're crazy."

His anger erupted, and he slammed the palm of his hand across her cheek. Sandy cried out.

"Don't call me that," He yelled. His anger dissipated as quick as it had occurred, and a pleased smile appeared on his grotesque face. He brushed her bangs from her eyes. "Let me put some lipstick on you and then you'll be pretty." He picked up the tube of pink lipstick from the bedside table and smeared it across Sandy's face from ear to ear. Then he clapped his hands together in delight. "You're beautiful! Now, we can have our tea party with our friends." He started gathering all the dolls from the shelf and lining them up beside her on the bed. "I'll be right back with the tea, Mommy. We're going to have so much fun."

Sandy watched him leave and fought the urge to scream. She kept her mouth shut, not wanting to upset him further, hoping to lure him into thinking he cowered her. So far it had worked, but now she knew she had to react. She was running out of time. Once again, she desperately pulled on the ropes tying her hands to the bedrails. No use.

He was back in a few moments, carrying a play tea set on a tray. A pink rose with thorns lay beside the set. He placed the tray on the table and turned to her with a stern look. "I'm going to untie one of your hands, Mommy, so you can drink your tea. After that, we can play naughty the way you like. Then, I'm going to kill you for the last time." He smiled pleasantly and untied the rope from around her right hand. Her quivering arm fell to her lap.

He turned back to the tea tray and without thinking of the consequences, Sandy's fingers grabbed the largest, unyielding plastic doll beside her. She slammed it hard against his head. He fell to the floor in a slump.

With her free hand, she worked on the knot holding her other hand. Frantic. Oh my God, hurry. Please. Please.

Finally, the rope gave, and she was free.

Staffer moaned.

Panicked, she jumped off the bed, took a step and screamed when his hand grabbed her ankle. She kicked out with her other foot, and he doubled over in pain. She kicked him in the side, again. "Die, you son of a bitch," she screamed. Turning, she ran. Out the door. Into the yard.

Then she was in the woods. Tears streamed down her face as she zigzagged through the trees, jumping over limbs and vines. Her lungs were pumping harsh air as she ran further and further into the trees. It was morning, but inside the thick stand of trees and brush it was pitch black, making it difficult to see where she was going.

Through her labored breathing, she heard crashing sounds not far behind her. He was still very much alive and coming for her.

Sobbing, she ran harder and faster. Her long legs pumped, and her lungs felt as if they would burst.

Suddenly, she tripped and fell, landing hard on her hands and knees. She heard a crash and a curse in the distance but closer than before. Moaning she forced her weak legs to lift her upright. She began running again. Desperate.

Had it been hours or mere minutes? She didn't know how far she'd gone or how much farther she had to go before she'd be out of the woods, but still, she kept running and thrashing her way toward freedom.

She could see daylight through the trees. She was close. So close. Oh God. A cry of utmost relief escaped.

Without warning, hands reached out and grabbed her.

Sandy screamed and kicked out. Her fist swung at her assailant's head. He held her tight.

"Sandy, stop it. It's me. Dobbs. Baby, you're safe. You're safe. They've caught him."

At the sound of his urgent voice, Sandy stopped fighting. Staring at him in disbelief, she grabbed Dobbs around the neck and held on for dear life while tears of relief and joy ran down her face. Dobbs held her close and rocked her back and forth.

She was safe.

CHAPTER TWENTY-EIGHT

Standing in her kitchen two weeks later, Tara nestled in Jake's arms, her head resting peacefully on his shoulder. He pulled her in closer. It was over. Staffer was finally behind bars, awaiting trial. He would never murder another woman. The jurors would make sure of it by requesting life without parole or the death sentence. From experience, she knew the presiding judge slammed his hammer down hard on convicted, habitual serial killers. The victims' family would finally have closure, including Walt Landers' limited family. During a wellness check, the police had found him dead in his apartment with a bullet hole in his forehead. Ben Staffer had admitted that he'd murdered his stepbrother to keep him silent. It would be an easy case for the prosecuting team and jurors to convict him. Yes. It was finally over.

Smiling, Tara glanced over at Dobbs and Sandy. Dobbs hadn't let her out of his sight since the madman had taken her. He'd requested a long vacation, and Chief Haynes had granted his request.

Dobbs and Sandy had spent every moment together since she'd been released from the hospital. Now, he was gazing at her with a goofy grin, so unlike the Dobbs she knew. She liked this side of him.

Tara turned her attention to retired Detective Brennan, Chief Haynes and Jackson, sitting next to Dobbs and Sandy at the new maple dining table she and Jake had chosen together. Her father's buddies had helped close a thirty-year-old case. They'd never have cracked the case as quickly as they had without the help of her friends, the veteran cops. Hopefully, her dad was looking down on them all with pride.

Tara's heart was full of happiness for the first time in years. Melinda and her husband Blake, Ben Marks, Cindy Tablor, both Jake's and Dobbs' parents and two couples who were colleagues of Jake's from the art gallery added to the small group sitting around the dining table. Lively conversation and wine flowed freely amongst their guests.

Jake sniffed into the air and brought her back to the present. "Um babe, unless you want to serve your beef lasagna burnt, you may want to check on it."

"Oh crap." She sprang from his arms and pulled the oven door open. A sigh of relief escaped her lips. Perfect. The dish was golden brown and bubbly. A scrumptious smell wafted past her nostrils as she pulled the main meal out of the oven and placed it on top of the new potholders lined up on the granite counter.

Mentally, she went over all her planned details for the meal. The salad was ready, and the garlic rolls were warm. The freshly baked chocolate cake was sitting on the counter waiting to be cut and served later. The table was set with her mother's for-guests-only best china. Everything was ready.

Tara glanced around and blinked back sudden tears. She had her loved ones there for the first dinner party she'd ever hosted with a meal she'd prepared and cooked. All by herself.

Well, with Jake's help. She loved that man.

Hopefully, her mother looked down from heaven, proud and smiling, too.

The next stand alone 'Tara' series.

TRUSTING TARA

Trusting Tara Excerpt

Chapter One

The December weather in Manhattan, New York was the worst they'd seen in twenty years. Heavy snow blanketed the sidewalks, roads, and roofs. Bundled up Christmas shoppers scurried from store to store, rushing to buy their gifts. Outside speakers mounted on the light poles played festive, holiday music. Santa Clauses in red suits sat on each street corner with excited children giggling and sitting on their laps, spouting off their Christmas wishes. A tall, brightly decorated Christmas tree was placed in Rockefeller Center for all to enjoy. Festive.

The person smirked, rubbed gloved hands together, and moved further into the shadows. Closer. Closer. Anticipating.

Two more weeks until Christmas. New York was alive and joyful. And, deadly.

* * *

Twenty-five-year old Shannon Reid, a young mother of four-year-old twin daughters, cuddled with them in their bedroom while she read them a Christmas bedtime story. When they drifted off to a sound sleep, she kissed their foreheads and tucked them into bed.

At eight p.m., she closed the door to their bedroom. With a smile of content, she went downstairs to pour herself a glass of wine. Her husband would soon return home from his business trip. He'd left Monday morning and had been gone for five days. Jason Reid was the love of her life and a devoted father to their beautiful daughters. She missed him terribly. And, she didn't like staying home alone with the children. Especially at night. She jumped at every sound.

She glanced around the massive kitchen that she'd lovingly decorated with a bright blue and silver backsplash, white ceramic floor and cabinet tile and over-the-top appliances. Their large, two-story home was located in one of the more elegant and gated neighborhoods of Manhattan. Jason was a wonderful provider.

Sipping her wine, she heard the key in the lock and the door open. She smiled, feeling like a giddy school girl even after five years of marriage. He was home. She slid off the stool and rushed into the living room lit only by the blinking Christmas tree lights to greet her husband. A scream of terror froze in her throat seconds before the bullet pierced her brain.

Connect with JERI LYNN STONE

I really appreciate you reading my books! I would love to hear from you. I appreciate all of my fans. I write for you and for my sanity.

If you enjoyed reading Terrorizing Tara please leave an honest review on Amazon.

Here are my social media coordinates:

Friend me on Facebook:
http://facebook.com/jerilynnstone
Follow me on Twitter:
http://twitter.com/jerlynstone
Subscribe to my blog:
http://www.jerilynnstone.blogspot.com
Visit my website:
http://www.jerilynnstone.wordpress.com

www.ingramcontent.com/pod-product-compliance
Lightning Source LLC
Chambersburg PA
CBHW070026120726
47909CB00003B/1076

Stolen at the Wildlife Sanctuary

Sanctuary

Linda Tassel Mysteries Book 3
by Eileen Charbonneau

Print ISBNs
Amazon print 978-0-2286-2574-2
BWL Print 978-0-2286-2575-9
Ingram Spark 978-0-2286-2576-6
Barnes & Noble

BWL Publishing Inc.

Books we love to write ...
Authors around the world.

http://bwlpublishing.ca